ANATOMY OF TERROR

A TALE OF TERROR FOR THE 21ST CENTURY

UNIVERSAL STUDIOS
MONSTERS

FRANKENSTEIN™

BY LARRY MIKE GARMON

D1018129

SCHOLASTIC INC.

New York   Toronto   London   Auckland   Sydney
Mexico City   New Delhi   Hong Kong   Buenos Aires

For my father, Royce Garmon, who taught me the value of hard work and family.

No part of this publication may be reproduced in whole or in part, or stored in a retrieval system, or transmitted in any form or by any means, electronic, mechanical, photocopying, recording, or otherwise, without written permission of the publisher. For information regarding permission, write to Scholastic Inc., Attention: Permissions Department, 555 Broadway, New York, NY 10012.

ISBN 0-439-30344-3

Designed by Peter Koblish

12 11 10 9 8 7 6 5 4 3 2 1   0 1 2 3 4 5 6/0
Printed in the U.S.A.
First Scholastic printing, November 2001

PROLOGUE

JUST BEFORE MIDNIGHT
SEASIDE CEMETERY

SAN TOMAS INLET
A DARK AND STORMY NIGHT

"Hurry up, you dolt! Do you want us to get caught?"

"No, Master," the hunchback replied through gritted teeth.

"Well, get underneath and push. I'll pull from up here." The master walked to the edge of the freshly dug grave. "But straighten it up first!"

"As you wish, Master."

Lightning flashed, revealing thick, dark clouds. For several seconds, the white tombstones surrounding the interlopers blazed like neon signs warning the grave robbers. The flash died and the luminous headstones faded into gray shadows in the moonless night.

The hunchback placed his right shoulder against the edge of the coffin and pushed with all the strength his deformed back and short, stocky legs would allow. He grunted.

Looking down into the freshly dug grave, the master watched in the flashing light as his hench-man struggled with the wooden coffin.

"We must hurry, Fritz," the master said. "The storm will be here soon."

With a final grunt, Fritz pushed the coffin up-right. It stood on end and then tilted as though it was going to fall.

"Catch it!" the master screamed. He made a grab for the edge of the upturned coffin, but missed. "It's falling."

"I've got it, Master!" Fritz yelled. Although his body and legs were short and stubby, his arms were long and powerful. He wrapped them around the coffin, his face pressing against the rotting wood. "No, my lovely. No, my dear. You shall not fall on Ol' Fritz." Once it was steady, Fritz let go of the cof-fin and leaned back. He kissed the death box like a long-lost friend. "Oh, no. Not on Ol' Fritz."

"If you're quite finished!"

Fritz looked up. Even though the sky was shrouded in dark clouds, his master's face shone forth with a pale glow. Fritz smiled. He loved his master and didn't let any abusive words diminish his admira-tion for the scientist who had saved his life.

"Yes, Master," Fritz said with a toothy grin. "I'm quite finished."

The master bent down and grabbed the handles on either side of the casket. "Okay: I'll pull and you push. Ready?"

Fritz knelt down and placed his hands under the edge of the box. "Ready, Master."

"On three." The master took a deep breath. "One . . . two . . . thr — whoa! Wait! Wait!"

The coffin shot up from the grave like a cork from a champagne bottle. The heavy casket hit the master in the chest and knocked him to the ground. Then it stood on end, tottering back and forth.

"No!" the master yelled. The coffin swayed toward the scientist. "No!" the master yelled again as the coffin began to fall toward him. He tried to scoot away, but it fell full onto his chest.

"Ugh!" the master groaned.

Fritz hopped out of the grave. He brushed the wet dirt from his clothes and looked around. "Master?" Fritz frowned. "Master? Where are you? Don't leave me alone, Master."

"I'm — under — the — coffin — Fritz," the master grunted.

Fritz ran to one side and bent over. Indeed, his master was pinned under the coffin, the heavy box flattening the scientist's nose.

"Now," the master grunted slowly. "If you'll gently tilt the box to one side, I'll slide out from underneath."

"Yes, Master," Fritz said with compliant glee. He gripped the edge of the box and then waited.

"What are you waiting for, Fritz?"

"Are you not going to count to three?"

The scientist grunted. "Just — tilt — the — COFFIN!"

With one swift move, Fritz threw the coffin off the scientist. It rolled several feet, finally stopping on its top.

Fritz slid his arm under the scientist's shoulders. "Here, let me help you, Master." Fritz's powerful arm catapulted the scientist bolt upright.

The scientist cried out as he shot toward the edge of the grave. "Fritz!"

Fritz grabbed the back of the scientist's black trench coat. "I have you, Master." Fritz pulled back and soon they were standing face-to-face — rather, Fritz's face was chest-high to his master.

The scientist tugged at his trench coat to straighten it. He brushed off the dirt and combed his fingers through his dark hair. He cleared his throat and said in a controlled voice, "Thank you, Fritz." He cocked one eyebrow and looked down at his henchman. The hunchback looked back at him like a puppy on Christmas morning. "Shall we put the coffin in the station wagon?"

Fritz laughed. "Yes, Master. In the station wagon."

They stood on either end and lifted the coffin, walking as quickly as the cumbersome box would let them. Minutes later, they were sliding it into the back of a battered 1965 Buick station wagon.

The master crawled in beside the coffin and quickly unscrewed the latches. The wet hinges creaked in protest as he pushed the lid up.

"Ah," he sighed with admiration. "This, Fritz, is

perfect. Dead only three days." He reached inside and lifted the arm of the dead teenager. "Perfect," he whispered. "Perfect." He closed the lid and scooted out of the back.

"Cover it up and close the door, Fritz," the master said.

Fritz threw an old, faded, tattered quilt over the coffin and slammed the rear door shut.

Lightning lit the night, the bursts reaching across the sky like long, thin fingers. The clouds had become thicker, darker.

Rain began to fall. Big, fat, heavy raindrops that felt like small stones. And they were cold. The scientist shuddered and quickly slid into the driver's seat. Fritz climbed into the passenger side.

"We did good, yes, Master?" Fritz asked eagerly.

"Yes, Fritz," the scientist said. He turned the ignition key and the old car came to life. "We will be able to complete our experiment with this body. His hands are perfect for my creature."

"Why, Master?" Fritz was like a child asking why the sky is blue.

"According to his obituary, he was the best pass receiver ever to play for Ponce de Leon High School. Ergo: good hands. My creature must be perfect in every way."

A flash of lightning washed out the interior of the car. Thunder blasted the night air, rattling the windows once more. Fritz cowered and hissed in fear.

The master looked out the windshield and up at the angry night sky. "Perhaps tonight we will prove once and for all that my theory of regeneration is correct. Four months of hard work, of digging up the graves of the newly dead. And we will complete our work tonight! Tonight life will conquer death!"

Fritz laughed — a wet, gurgling laugh. "Life!" Fritz repeated, just as lightning flashed again.

Even the scientist laughed this time.

Fritz turned on the radio. The old tube radio crackled to life. He twisted the dial until it landed on his favorite station. A concertina whined through the cracked speakers as a foreign voice sang out words that Fritz did not understand.

The scientist put the car in gear and slowly drove down the cemetery's narrow lane in darkness. He frowned. "I'll never understand what you find so interesting about rancheros. American country music is bad enough. Mexican country music is even worse!" The scientist shook his head. "The next time I steal a car, I'm going to make sure that it has an FM radio."

"The music is beautiful, Master," Fritz replied gravely.

Moments later, they were at the exit. The scientist looked both ways and then drove onto the streets of the living.

Living? the scientist thought. *Life!* He laughed to himself. *After tonight, medical science will have to come up with a new definition for life!* After tonight, he would achieve a fame he had never dreamed of in his other life — his life of dull grays, blackest black, and washed-out whites.

They drove for several blocks, finally turning the car onto Beachfront Road, toward an old warehouse they'd converted into a morgue.

The ranchero music snapped and crackled through the speakers, giving the song a metallic, reedy sound.

The scientist smiled. *Tonight I will bring my creature to life and all those fools will see. They'll see!*

Detective Mike Turner yawned. He placed the palm of his hands against the roof of the car and pushed up. His spine popped and cracked. "Ah," he said with a sigh. Being short had its advantages. A taller man would have had to get out of the car to stretch.

He pressed a button on his wristwatch. The time flashed at him in a bluish hue — 00:13.

I've got to set this thing back to regular time, he thought. *Military time can be annoying. Good thing I'm not superstitious. Two zeros and unlucky 13: Can't get much worse than that!* He pushed two more buttons and the watch finally read 12:13.

Superstition based on numbers was just one of Turner's eccentricities. Superstition based on weather was another, and, of course, the typical late fall San Tomas weather wasn't helping his nerves. The storm had sneaked up on San Tomas Inlet like a cat preying on an unsuspecting bird. Big, fat rain drops drummed on the windshield of Turner's car. *At least I'm dry.*

Turner had been sitting in the car for over eight hours, watching the empty warehouse, waiting for signs of life. Several days earlier, he'd gotten a tip from a reliable informant that the deserted warehouse was being used as a chop shop. He had scouted the warehouse for four nights and had not seen any signs of activity. On the first night of his stakeout, he had stealthily investigated the outside of the warehouse. The windows had been covered with black paint, so he could not see what was inside. He didn't have enough evidence to get a search warrant, so now he was sitting for hours, hoping to catch someone pulling into the warehouse in a stolen car. Then he'd have probable cause to enter the warehouse without a warrant.

Stolen cars were a constant problem in San Tomas Inlet, especially during the tourist season. And car thieves loved to take their stolen wares to a chop shop: a place where the car would be taken apart, piece by piece, and then sold for its parts. More money and harder to trace.

Turner fumbled through the crumpled wrappers and boxes that littered the car, hoping to find a morsel of food. He couldn't believe he was still hungry. Stakeouts always made him ravenous, even though he was doing little more than just sitting. On this night, he had eaten enough food for three men in the eight hours he'd been waiting. Good thing he had a fast metabolism. At 5'6", 130 pounds, and thirty years of age, Detective Mike Turner still looked like a high school student. In fact, surrounding law enforcement agencies often employed Turner to go undercover to find high school teens involved in crime.

Turner didn't mind his size or his youthful looks. It was better than the middle-age paunch that had already grown on some of his fellow officers. Someday his juvenile face would give way to the wrinkled ravages of time and weather. But for now, he was happy to be just as he was.

Turner was still hunting for food when he heard a car speed past him.

He sat up in his seat. A battered old station wagon with two passengers had passed him. The right rear taillight was burnt out. Turner had to check his first instinct, which was to stop the car and give the driver a warning about the bad light. He wasn't there to make petty traffic stops.

Turner pulled out a small pair of night-vision binoculars, training them on the dimly lit license plate. He quickly committed the number to memory. Holding the binoculars with his left hand, he used his right to type the license number into the police car's computer. He hit the ENTER button with his pinky and waited.

The wagon pulled up to the large double doors of the warehouse. The passenger door opened.

"What the —" Turner said out loud. In the dim yellow hue of the station wagon's headlights, he saw a large monkey get out, waddle up to the double doors, and swing them open. "Is that a man?" The apelike creature waved a long, thick arm, and the wagon slowly ambled into the warehouse.

Lightning flashed just as the ape-man was closing the doors. Turner gasped. Through his binoculars he could now clearly see that the creature was indeed a man. A man with a twisted mouth that pointed down in a perpetual frown, a hump protruding up from his left shoulder, and a shock of red hair that waved wildly in the stormy wind.

A beep echoed through the car. Turner glanced down at the computer screen. In bright, digital letters he got the answer he had wanted: The car had been reported stolen.

Then he frowned. Why would someone steal a 1965 Buick station wagon? There was no value in it.

Old or not, the fact that he had just witnessed a stolen car being driven into the warehouse gave him probable cause to investigate the warehouse and its contents — and to question the two men who were now inside the building.

Turner turned on the engine but left his lights off. He slowly drove along the same path the stolen car had taken minutes before. He was in no hurry. Speeding up to the entrance and slamming on the brakes would ruin the element of surprise.

He stopped the car twenty yards from the warehouse's entrance. He pulled his .357 magnum from its shoulder holster and checked the barrel: six bullets. Hopefully, he wouldn't need any of them. He made sure that the radio hanging on his side was off. He didn't want any sudden noise to startle the two men as he approached them.

Turner decided against calling for backup until he was sure he had some illegal activity going on. He was still taking a ribbing from his colleagues because of an incident a few months earlier. He had had several officers search the old Carfax Hotel, looking for vampires. That was the last time he would listen to a couple of teenage boys.

The detective gently opened the door and stepped from the car. Heavy, cold rain hit him in the face. He crouched and ran up to the metal building.

Legally, Turner could have just burst through the door, but that would have been foolish. He didn't know what was on the other side. Kicking in a door and yelling, "Hands up! This is the police!" worked in the movies, but in reality, such a move got you killed quickly.

Turner made his way back to the large double doors. He would have to chance opening one slightly to see inside. He took a breath, held it, and moved the door. It was heavy but well-balanced, and slid open just an inch.

Lightning flashed, thunder roared, and the cold, heavy rain continued to pound the earth. Turner decided to wait for the next flash and peal of thunder, then open the door enough for him to slide through. The thunder would mask any noise the opening door would make.

He didn't have to wait long. Lightning flashed and almost immediately, thunder roared. Turner pushed the door open and slipped in.

The light blinded him. He crouched, his gun raised in front of him. The station wagon was a few yards ahead. He duck-walked to the back of the car and leaned against it. He quickly poked his head around and then back. He didn't see the two men who had driven into the warehouse.

The warehouse was divided in two sections by the same corrugated steel siding that wrapped around the outside. The car sat in the smaller section. Turner glanced into the back of the station wagon, hoping to find some evidence of stolen-car activity. Nothing but dirt and mud.

Turner tiptoed to the door separating the two sections. This didn't look like any chop shop he had ever seen before. No parts lying about. No grease on the floors. No car skeletons. Nothing to indicate that the two men were in the business of selling parts from stolen vehicles.

He placed his hand on the doorknob and slowly turned the brass handle. The door opened easily and soundlessly. Turner peered in. A small, bare bulb suspended high from the ceiling lit the room in a garish glare. Turner listened, but didn't hear a sound. He slipped through the door into the harshly lit room. On tiptoes, Turner approached the opposite side and found a second door. He opened it slowly, and held his breath as he heard voices.

He couldn't tell what the two men were saying, but each had a very distinctive voice. One voice was smooth and silky, refined and commanding. The second was like tires on gravel on a hot, dry day.

This was no stolen-car ring. Turner began to wonder if perhaps he hadn't stumbled into something more dangerous. He began to regret his decision not to call for backup.

As before, a single bulb sent a harsh circle of light into the center of the room, but kept the rest of the room in darkness. The two men were standing in the center of the circle of light, in front of an oblong box that rested on two sawhorses. One man was tall and thin, wearing what appeared to be a black trench coat. The second was the apelike man who had opened the double doors.

Turner moved the door ever so slowly until he had just enough room to slide through. He pressed his back against the wall and gripped his .357 magnum in both hands. Their low mumbling still prevented him from hearing what the two men were discussing, but all of their attention was directed at the open box.

Turner had his police radio on his left hip. He decided to sneak up on the men, order them to the floor, and then use his radio to call for backup. He took a deep, silent breath and then headed toward the men. When he was ten yards from them, he trained the powerful gun on the apelike man. Of the two men, Turner was more apprehensive about the smaller, stronger-looking man.

"Police. Hands up and lay —"

Startled, both men spun around and stared into the deadly barrel of the .357.

Turner gasped, then gagged. He was a seasoned police officer who had seen his share of accident victims, gory gunshot wounds, and mutilated bodies. But no matter how much he saw of the wicked and horrible things that one person could do to another, he never got used to it, and he would always react when he came across such atrocities.

The taller, thin man, the man he had deemed less dangerous, held within each of his own hands a pair of freshly chopped-off hands.

"Don-don't move," Turner stuttered, the pistol steady on the two men.

His mind raced. Pages of recent reports flipped through his mind. Grave robbing. There had been several reports over the past four months in the usually sleepy resort town of San Tomas Inlet. It occurred to him that this was no ordinary chop shop.

Turner lowered his free hand to his radio. It crackled to life.

Lightning flashed again, snaking its way through

a skylight high in the ceiling and falling upon the box.

Turner gasped. It wasn't just a box. In the brief two seconds that the lightning illuminated the room, Turner saw that it was a coffin, and within the coffin was the corpse of a teenager. A teenager who was now without hands.

A low, guttural growl echoed off the metal walls. Turner pointed his gun directly at the apelike man, whose yellow, rotted teeth were bared like a dog's. The hunchback's eyes glowed with fury.

With a quickness belying his short, stocky body, the apelike man sprang at Turner and slammed into the small detective.

Turner fell to the floor. The .357 came to life. Fire from the muzzle exploded at the apelike man. Turner saw a strip of skin rip as the bullet creased the left side of the ape-man's head.

The misshapen man screamed. Although the bullet had only grazed him, the power of the missile jerked his head to the right and his body twisted in response. He landed on the floor next to Turner.

Turner rolled to his right and onto his knees, aiming the barrel of the .357 at the middle of the ape-man's chest.

"No!" screamed the tall man.

Still holding the gun on the hunchback, Turner slowly rose to his feet.

The hunchback, too, was on his feet. He sprang

again. Again Turner fired, but this time the hunchback was ready. The man-beast twisted his body slightly, and the bullet missed completely. He tackled Turner once more, and again Turner smashed into the floor. But this time, he wasn't so lucky. He hit with such force that his head slammed into the concrete. He coughed up blood.

The hunchback was on him, pounding both sides of his face with his fists. Turner fought to remain conscious. The hunchback grabbed Turner by the collar and lifted the detective's shoulders. Then he head-butted the detective.

A fiery explosion erupted inside Turner's brain. A curtain of darkness began to lower itself over his befuddled mind. The tall, thin man came into his eyesight. Both men stood over Turner. The thin man still held the armless hands within his own.

"Fritz," the tall man said.

"Yes, Master," the hunchback replied.

"I think I have found a better pair of hands." The tall man dropped the hands he'd just severed from the occupant of the oblong box. He knelt and lifted the detective's limp right arm. "Yes, these hands are much better. Bring me my scalpel, Fritz."

The last thing Turner saw before slipping into unconsciousness was the toothy, rotten grin of the hunchback.

CHAPTER ONE

TUESDAY AFTERNOON, 1:45 P.M.
MS. BASHARA'S ENGLISH CLASS, ROOM 244
PONCE DE LEON HIGH SCHOOL

Joe Motley squirmed in his seat. He felt his body growing numb. The small, hard plastic chair was uncomfortable.

Joe glanced at his watch. He wondered if time could move any more slowly. He looked out the window. The sky was dark. The storm had brought heavy rain and a slight fall chill to the resort town. Joe had wanted to go skateboarding with his best friend, but the weather wasn't being very cooperative. In a couple more hours, the clouds would unleash the same spectacular thunder and lightning storm that had hit the night before.

He looked back down at his literature textbook. The words blurred into meaningless strings. He liked reading just about any kind of literature, he just didn't like *having* to read it and then analyze and synthesize and compartmentalize or any other *-ize* his English teacher could think of. Joe didn't know what was worse: fighting monsters or writing essays.

Joe crossed his arms and leaned on his desk. Just a little over four months ago, he had inadvertently released six monsters from Universal Studios classic horror movies. He and his best friend, Robert Hardin, along with another friend, Nina Nobriega, had just wanted to test the prototype of a new three-dimensional projector created by the Universal Studios Florida Research and Development team. It was Joe who had modified the binary code and rewritten some of the program errors he had found in the Universal programming. And it was Joe who had transferred the six classic horror movies to special 3-D DVD discs. And like something out of a horror movie, a bolt of lightning had struck Nina's house, snaked through the electrical wiring, and exploded inside the projector and the DVD drive that held the six movies.

Their first encounter had been with the suave and deadly Count Dracula, who had been intent on turning Nina's friend Angela into his immortally dead bride. Joe had used his keen knowledge of computer programming and technology to turn Nina's digital camcorder into an electromagnetic-spectrum vacuum cleaner and sucked Count Dracula back into his black-and-white world. That had been easy.

Or at least, it had been easy compared to what came next — capturing the Wolf Man. First they had discovered that not only had the werewolf escaped his classic movie, but that the ancient gypsy from the werewolf legend had slipped into reality, too. Plus, the modified camcorder hadn't worked until Nina had evoked a little ancient mysticism to help defeat the monster.

Science and magic had worked together on the Wolf Man. Joe smiled: He felt like a modern-day electronic alchemist.

In each battle, they had come close to either succumbing to the allure of the monsters, or losing their lives. Fortunately, when they had defeated the classic monsters, everything seemed to turn back to normal. Close the book, turn off the projector, eject the DVD, and you're back in reality. Except that he had seen the human form of the werewolf and the gypsy again — *after* they'd used the camera on them. That still puzzled Joe. He frowned as he looked down at his textbook. Joe had double-checked the special 3-D DVD, and Larry Talbot and the gypsy woman from *The Wolf Man* were right where they were supposed to be — in their Universal Studios movie. Why, then, had Joe, Nina, and Bob seen their human forms, Deputy Barnes and Wilma Winokea?

He and Captain Bob had talked about it for hours, but had no answer. Joe had decided to double-check the DVD's electronic programming. Maybe he had missed something in the binary code. Maybe the program he had designed had become corrupted somehow.

He also wondered just which monster would appear next and how they would defeat it. The remaining candidates were the Creature from the

Black Lagoon, the Bride of Frankenstein, Frankenstein, and the Mummy. Neither Joe, Nina, nor Bob
knew which one they would have to fight; Joe just
hoped they would be ready when the time came.
And he hoped the camcorder would work as easily
as it had on Count Dracula.

Joe looked over at his best friend, Bob. The desks
were arranged in a circle, and Captain Bob sat directly across from him. Joe smiled. He wondered if
it was possible for Bob to read any more dramatically than he was at that moment. At least Captain
Bob could read well. Most of the students in the
class, when asked to read, did so with all the enthu-
siasm of a prisoner being led to death row. And although Captain Bob and Ms. Bashara didn't get
along, she always called on him to read because he
didn't have to follow the words with his finger.

Captain Bob's eyes darted back and forth over
the words of the text, and his voice rose dramatically.
His face twisted and distorted with each phrase.

Joe laughed to himself. He knew what was coming. Captain Bob loved an audience. And he loved
to get under Ms. Bashara's skin.

*"I could bear those hypocritical smiles no longer! I
felt that I must scream or die! — and now — again! —
hark! louder! louder! louder! LOUDER!"*

Captain Bob jumped up from his seat and darted
to the center of the room. He dropped his book on
the floor. There was a loud pop as the heavy literature book slammed onto the hard tile. Several stu-

dents gasped and a few screamed. A slumbering student only groaned and snorted.

" 'Villains,' I shrieked, 'dissemble no more! I admit the deed!' " — Captain Bob fell to his knees and pantomimed ripping up wooden floor planks — " 'tear up the planks! — here, here! — it is the beating of his hideous heart!' "

Captain Bob raised his right arm. His fingers pulsed in and out as though he were holding on to a real beating heart. His head dropped.

The class sat in silence. Then Joe applauded. A couple of students joined him.

"Encore," one girl said.

Without missing a beat, Captain Bob looked at the girl and winked.

The bell rang, and the students ran for the door before they could see their English teacher's reaction.

Captain Bob grabbed his book, jumped to his feet, and joined the escaping students.

"Robert Hardin!"

Bob froze in place. That voice. That tone. That imperative. If Ms. Bashara had been on the *Titanic* and had yelled at the iceberg, the chunk of frozen mountain would have moved out of the ship's way.

"Smooth move, Captain Boob," Joe whispered as he quickly walked past his best friend.

"Thanks," Bob answered sarcastically. He turned slowly. Ms. Bashara still sat at her desk, her hands folded across the open literature book. Her lips were pursed, and she drummed her fingers on the book.

"Yes, Ms. Bashara," Bob said with a lilt. "May I help you?"

The drumming continued. Ms. Bashara sighed.

"I'm going to be late to my next class, Ms. Bashara." Bob turned to leave.

"Just one minute, Hardin!"

Bob turned around again. *Here it comes,* he thought. *The Sentence.* You know: Your parents have The Lecture and your teachers have The Sentence, that endless string of words that teachers believe will magically change a student from class clown to star pupil. Bob had heard it so often that he was able to recite it word for word, phrase for phrase, tone for tone with Ms. Bashara, Ponce de Leon High's reigning Queen of The Sentence.

"Hardin, you have a lot of talent and intelligence and it's a shame that you waste it on juvenile displays like the one I just witnessed."

"Yes, Ms. Bashara," Bob replied as sheepishly as possible. He turned to leave.

"Annnd —"

Oh, no! Two Sentences. This was torture. Bob turned around.

"— you would do well to channel that talent and intelligence into more fruitful endeavors."

"Yes, Ms. Bashara." Again he turned to leave.

"Sooo —"

No! Bob screamed inwardly. He hadn't committed such a grave offence as to deserve Three Sentences.

"— I've volunteered you for the freshman class play." The drumming stopped. Ms. Bashara closed her literature book, folded her hands across it, and eyed Bob Hardin.

Bob began to protest, but Ms. Bashara raised her hand. "Or —"

And that was all Ms. Bashara had to say. Not only did Bob get Three Sentences, but he was also whammied with the dreadful Or, which could be anything from a call to your parents to after-school detention.

"Yes, Ms. Bashara."

"You can pick up a rehearsal schedule on your way out the door. I think you will make an excellent Julius Caesar."

"Yes, Ms. Bashara." Bob sighed and slouched out the door.

"Well?" Joe said as Bob joined him at the water fountain.

Bob grimaced.

"You get The Sentence?"

"Worse."

Joe's eyebrows raised. "Two Sentences?"

Bob sniffed.

Joe whistled. "Three Sentences?"

"And an Or!"

Joe chuckled. "She's really ticked at you, buddy. I told you not to put that fake dead rat in her lunch bag."

"She didn't know I did it."

Joe laughed. "Oh, really? We've only been in high school for three months and already the teachers have your number, buddy."

Bob turned and smacked into what felt like a brick wall. He hit the slick tile with his butt and slid along the floor. His hat tilted forward and covered his eyes.

"Watch where you're going, freshman!" came a deep voice from above.

Bob looked up, squinting past the rim of his hat. Oscar Morales glared down his long nose at him. Oscar was a monster linebacker on the Ponce football team — and sometimes it seemed as though that position was named just for him.

Bob stood with Joe's help.

"I said watch where you're going, freshman," Morales repeated. This time his words were slow and deliberate.

"He wants you to apologize," Joe whispered.

"I know what he wants," Bob replied, straightening his hat.

Oscar glared down at the short freshman. "Well?" he said, balling his fists.

Several students had stopped to watch the encounter. Bob eyed them and then looked at Oscar. Over the years, being short had taught Bob to be tough. The shortest kid and the newest kid always had to prove themselves. And unfortunately, this year Bob was both rolled into one.

"This is not the time," Joe whispered, darting his eyes toward the crowd.

Bob looked at the crowd. Half the Ponce Bulldogs defensive line stared back at him, and they were all just as big and and ugly as Oscar. Joe was right.

Bob flicked his captain's hat from his head so quickly that Oscar flinched. Then he bent over into a deep bow like a bad actor at curtain call. "O, forgivest me, great one!"

"You making fun of me, you twerp?" Oscar demanded. "I'll fold you up and put you in my back pocket!"

From the corner of his eye, Bob saw Ms. Bashara step from her classroom. Bob raised an eyebrow and smiled.

"Then you'll have more brains in your pocket than you do in your head," Bob replied, smiling sardonically.

A general "Oooo" rose from the crowd. Oscar reached out for Bob, but the freshman was too quick for him. He ducked under Oscar's arm and darted into the crowd.

Oscar began after him. "Why you little—"

"Oscar Morales!" came Ms. Bashara's sternest voice. "You told me yesterday you'd have that essay turned in by this morning!"

"But, Ms. Bashara, we've had practice, and—"

Ms. Bashara cut him off short. "I don't want to hear any excuses, Morales. You're already on academic probation. Now get into class. I better have that essay by the end of the hour, or . . ." Her voice faded away as she led the big senior into her classroom.

"He's gonna kill you, you know that, right?" Joe asked as he and Bob started down the hallway again.

"He's got to catch me first, and I have no intention of getting caught."

Joe shook his head. "You have a regular talent for getting yourself in trouble, you know that?"

"Let's just get to biology, Mr. Perfect."

"Certainly," Joe replied. "We're dissecting today. Ought to be cool." They started down the crowded hallway toward the science lab.

"Yeah, but I got a new lab partner. That new kid."

"Who? I haven't seen him."

"Dr. James gave me his name yesterday."

"Well, what is it?"

"I can't remember it. City Tree Joe."

"City Tree Joe?"

"Yeah. His first name's like a city. Seattle, Denver, Dallas. I don't know."

"Where's your lab slip?"

"Oh, yeah," Bob said and dug in his front pocket. He pulled out a crumpled paper, a fake smashed cockroach with yellow bug juice, and lint.

"What's the plastic cockroach for?" Joe asked with a knowing nod.

"This kid in fourth period. He's been razzing me because my mom and I live in a mobile home. So, he's going to find a little surprise in his lunch."

"You got a thing for pranking other people's lunches, don't ya?" Joe grabbed the crumpled piece of paper and unfolded it. He rolled his eyes. "Francisco."

"Yeah. I told you it was the name of a city. Francisco Tree-joe."

Joe rolled his eyes again. "You're not passing Spanish, are you?"

"How do you know that?" Bob asked, puzzled.

"It's not pronounced Tree-joe. It's T-R-E-J-O."

"Yeah," Bob said, grabbing the paper and looking at it. "Tree-joe."

"The *J* is pronounced like an *H* and the T-R-E is pronounced like *tray*. Tray-ho. Francisco Tray-ho."

Bob shoved the paper back into his pocket. "Whatever. I just don't want to break in a new lab partner. I don't know why I got assigned the new kid."

"Probably because you set Megan McMahan's fake hair on fire with the Bunsen burner and everyone else refuses to work with you."

"Yeah. No one has a sense of humor these days."

"How much do you still owe Megan for burning up her sixty-dollar weave?"

"Forty bucks! That's another thing. Sixty bucks

for fake hair. I'll shave my dog and weave her a do for twenty bucks." Bob laughed mischievously.

"I think you've done enough, buddy."

"Hi, Skinny," Bob said to the display skeleton hanging in the corner as they entered the lab. He saluted the skeleton and then sat down on a stool.

"Please take your hat off, Captain Bob," Dr. James said from the front of the room. The teacher had his back to the class as he wrote on the antiquated chalkboard, and he didn't even bother to turn around.

"Yes, Dr. James." Bob took off his battered yacht captain's hat, folded it, and placed it in his back pocket. Of all the teachers at Ponce de Leon High School, only Dr. James called Bob by his preferred name — Captain Bob. For that favor, Bob rarely misbehaved in Dr. James's biology class.

Rarely. Sometimes Bob thought he could still smell the acrid scent of the burning yak hair as Megan McMahan's weave dipped into the Bunsen burner he had just lit. She was showing off one of her dance team moves, bending over backward. Captain Bob shook his head. The burner incident was an accident. *What in blazes was she doing leaning back, anyway?*

But in the three short months of his high school career, Captain Bob had earned such a reputation for being a prankster that when something really was an accident, no one believed him.

Bob just shrugged it off. He had forty dollars to go in repaying Megan. That meant more hours at the Beach Burger and fewer hours on his computer at home or skateboarding with Joe.

"Okay, class," Dr. James began, turning to face the class, "today we are going to explore the marvelous world of amphibious anatomy. Now if each of you would pair up with your respective lab partners, we'll begin."

"That's so gross," Megan spoke up from the back of the room. Bob turned. Megan stared right past him. "Cutting up an innocent little frog is inhumane."

"You're mixing your metaphors," Bob said.

Megan glared at him. "I'm not even using a metaphor."

"That accounts for the smell," Captain Bob said, waving his hand in front of his nose.

The class burst out laughing.

Megan stomped her foot. "That doesn't even make sense. You people are just encouraging rude behavior!"

Bob could tell that Dr. James was suppressing a laugh. He knew that his statement made absolutely no sense, but it was so ridiculous that the others laughed. He'd perfected the technique in junior high.

Dr. James rapped his knuckles on his desk. "That's enough, class. Megan has a point. Vivisection is a hot topic in some scientific circles. With the advances in computer technology, many schools, including universities, have opted to use computer-generated models instead of live dead subjects."

Bob smiled at the oxymoron. He made a mental note to remember that one.

"But haven't you ever wanted to look beyond the clouds, the stars? To know what causes the trees to bud? What changes the darkness into light?" Dr. James walked from behind his desk and began to wander among the lab tables. "Haven't you ever wanted to just reach out and touch what is real, what you can smell, what you can taste? Computers are a great invention, but they can only offer you simulated reality. You could learn about animal anatomy on a computer." He looked at Megan. "But isn't that like a dancer learning to dance without ever taking a step? Computers, books, movies, television — they all have their places. Unfortunately, in today's culture, they have misplaced what is real and tangible in life." He stopped by Bob's table and looked at the freshman. "Not me. I want to discover what the secret of life is. I want to discover why we die. If I could discover just one of those things, what eternity is, for example, I wouldn't care if the whole world thought I was crazy!"

The teacher smiled at Bob. Bob liked Dr. James because the teacher was as short and stocky as he was, and didn't care what anybody thought of him. Just like Bob himself. Dr. James always wore an old-fashioned lab coat that buttoned up the left side rather than up the middle, and it was always stained and a little tattered. Not unlike Bob's hat.

Dr. James returned to the front of the room. "Ready, class?"

The students pulled their plastic lab coats from under their tables and noisily put them on. All except for Megan, who only grimaced and pouted.

"Now," Dr. James said, "let me introduce you to Mr. *Rana catesbeiana*." In one hand he held a big dead bullfrog dripping formaldehyde; in the other, a scalpel. "In order to discover the secrets of life, we must first discover the secrets of death."

He took the scalpel and gently ran the blade down the frog from below the chin to the stomach. Formaldehyde oozed from inside it. Several students squealed and laughed.

Bob looked around the room for his new lab partner. He noticed a thin boy sitting at a lab table next to Skinny. The boy looked down at his knees. Bob sighed and shrugged. He didn't like the idea of having a lab partner. He wanted the frog all to himself. But he also knew that Dr. James wouldn't allow him to work by himself.

"My name's Bob. Captain Bob," Bob said as he walked up to the boy. "You must be Francisco Tree — I mean, Tray-ho."

The boy looked up. His eyes were as dark as his hair and they penetrated into Bob's eyes. He wore a large baggy T-shirt and blue jeans with red sneakers. "Hello," the boy said, his accent thick.

"My table's over here, Francisco." Bob waved with his arm and walked toward it.

"Call me Trey," the boy replied, following Bob. "Francisco sounds like I ought to have my own zip code."

Bob smiled. A sense of humor. Maybe the kid would be a cool lab partner after all.

To Bob's surprise and chagrin, Trey picked up the scalpel and began the first incision on the frog. He was quick and neat and before Bob realized it, his new lab partner had the bullfrog's intestines sitting in the lab tray.

CHAPTER TWO
STILL TUESDAY, 2:45 P.M.
MRS. HOVING'S HUMANITIES CLASS, ROOM 111

"How long will the exhibition be in town?" Nina Nobriega asked.

"Well, let's see." Mrs. Hoving peered over her bifocals at a brochure she held in her hands. "From December tenth through February nineteenth." She looked over the edge of the brochure at Nina and the rest of the class. "That's quite a long time."

"How long should we volunteer for?" Nina asked.

"They have graduate assistants helping with the exhibition and would like any high school students interested in Western civilization and humanities to volunteer as much time as they can spare." Mrs. Hoving smiled at Nina.

"Cool," Nina said, raising her eyebrows. "That includes an Egyptian exhibit, doesn't it?"

"Of course. Then I can put you down for — ?" Mrs. Hoving said, picking up a pencil.

"Let me check my calendar," Nina said. "But I think I can work just about anytime they need me."

"Calendar?" Stacy McDonald said. "You have a

social life? The only people I see you hanging with are those two stupid freshmen boys and that Angela chick whose sister is a vampire freak or whatever." Several other girls giggled.

Nina grimaced. For some reason, Stacy had decided to pick on her for the last two weeks. Like Nina's parents, Stacy's parents were rich. Unlike Stacy, though, Nina had a level head about it.

"Well?" Stacy said, extending a challenge for Nina to retort.

Nina smiled. What would Captain Bob do in a situation like this? Probably throw up on the chick. Nina laughed, then stopped herself. "Does Camryn Manheim know you stole her wardrobe?"

Stacy's eyes widened and her jaw dropped. "Are you saying I'm fat?"

Nina turned around, crossed her arms, and smiled.

"All right, class. That's enough. Let's get back to the volunteers for the Western Civilization and Humanities Exhibition coming to San Tomas."

Stacy raised her hand, but she didn't wait to be called on. "Mrs. Hoving, Nina just said that I'm fat."

Mrs. Hoving looked perplexed. "Really? What's wrong with that? Isn't that supposed to be cool with you kids today or something?"

Stacy gasped just as the bell rang. She bolted up and stomped from the room, a small clique of girls chasing after her.

Nina decided to remain seated long enough for

the hallways to clear. She didn't want to meet up with Stacy and her gaggle. She had other business after school that was much more important.

"Did I say something wrong?" Mrs. Hoving said with a shrug of her shoulders. "I thought phat was a compliment these days."

Nina stood and walked up to the teacher's desk. "Yes, it is, Mrs. Hoving."

A look of exasperation crossed the teacher's face. "I just don't understand kids' jargon. One day a word is cool and the next day it's an insult. I'll stick to my Funk and Wagnall's, thank you very much." Mrs. Hoving stood. She was short and stout and about as mean as a kitten. "I'm glad you're interested in working at the exhibit, Nina."

"I'm thinking about majoring in anthropology, Mrs. Hoving. I've always had an interest in ancient history."

Mrs. Hoving looked at Nina over the top of her bifocals. "You've got the brains, and from the work I've seen you do here, you have the desire. But you're still young." The woman smiled. "No need to rush into anything. Here's the information you'll need, plus a parental permission form."

"Thank you." Nina took the forms but she didn't move. She glanced at her watch. She wondered if the gaggle was waiting for her outside.

"Yes? Anything else?" Mrs. Hoving shoveled a load of papers into a canvas book bag and locked her desk.

Nina took a deep breath. "How large is the Egyptian portion? Will there be a mummy?"

"I think it's a large part of it." She looked at the brochure again. "Says here there's a mummy but doesn't explain anything about it," Mrs. Hoving said. She finished packing up, took her glasses off her nose, and looked at Nina. "I really don't want to be late for my dance class."

"Cool," Nina said with a large smile, happy for an opportunity to continue the conversation as they walked out into the hall. "You take dance lessons?"

"Humph! Take dance lessons? My dear, I *teach* dance lessons." And as if on cue, Mrs. Hoving pretended to grab an invisible partner and did an improvised fox trot down the hallway and out the door of the school.

Nina laughed, but quickly stopped when she heard a noise behind her.

In the past four months, Nina had battled Count Dracula and the Wolf Man. She was prepared to fight the other monsters she and her two freshmen friends had released. What she didn't want was a face-off with Stacy McDonald. She would just as soon have the fangs of some horrible creature bearing down on her than have Stacy up in her face in the school hallway.

Nina tensed and took a deep breath. The door at the end of the hallway was too far for her to run. She'd just have to turn and face Stacy and the gaggle. She spun around.

"Hocus pocus locus!" Bob said, his fingers waving in front of Nina's eyes.

Nina's cheeks puffed out in exasperation and she slapped his hands away.

"Bob Hardin, one of these days I'm going to forget I'm a lady and punch you in your sinuses!"

"I've already forgotten you're a lady, so take your best shot." Captain Bob jumped back into a defensive martial arts position, one leg crooked up and hands in a not-quite-real karate position. "Whaaaa!" he squealed.

Nina was tempted to throw her books at him. The humanities text alone was heavy enough to knock him into a coma.

"Your fly's open," she said, brushing past him.

"What?" Bob turned away and checked himself. Then he made a face. He had forgotten he was wearing sweatpants. "Hey! No fair."

"Nice one," Joe said, raising his palm.

Nina slapped it. "Thanks, big guy." She flipped back her brown hair and adjusted the books in her arms into a more comfortable position.

"So, what's up?" Joe asked. He and Nina started toward the exit.

"Yeah," Bob said as he trotted to join them. "Kathy Darby handed me a note in biology just as I was getting into the inner workings of Mr. *Rana catesbeiana.*"

Joe laughed so loudly that Nina glanced at him in surprise. The freshman was 6'1" and 215 pounds, but very mild-mannered. However, Nina suspected that if Joe ever really got mad enough to let loose, the ground would quake and the sky would split open.

"Yeah," Joe said. "Captain Boob here thought it was a love note from Kathy. You should have seen the puppy-dog eyes he had when he took it from her."

Whenever Bob did not have anything clever or witty or sarcastic to say to anybody, he just ignored them. This was often the case with his best friend's comments. He ignored Joe and said, "So, what's up? We've got a Forensics Club meeting with Detective Turner."

"I don't think so," Nina said.

"Why?" Bob asked.

"Detective Turner is in the hospital. He was found in a warehouse last night, unconscious. He's in intensive care."

A look of astonishment came over Joe. "What happened?" he said.

"No one's sure."

"How did you find out?" Bob said.

Nina frowned. "Who cares how I found out? The important thing is that Detective Turner has been seriously injured, and I found this in last night's paper." She held out a small clipping.

Joe took the clipping before Bob could grab it. His eyes quickly scanned the article.

"What is it?" Bob said. Joe continued to read.

"What is it?" Bob asked again. He grabbed the clipping, and the newspaper tore.

"Freshmen," Nina muttered.

Bob held the two pieces of the clipping together and finished reading. He whistled. "You guys thinking what I'm thinking?"

"I doubt it," Nina said. "We're not that confused when we think."

Bob frowned. "Hardy-har-har."

Joe said, "A brain has been stolen from the School of Medicine. I'll give you odds it's Dr. Frankenstein!"

"Only a sucker would take that bet," Nina replied, glancing at Bob. "Not only that," she added, dropping her voice to a whisper. The boys leaned in closer. "But they found Detective Turner in an abandoned warehouse. And in the warehouse they found six corpses. What they didn't find were all the body parts to those corpses."

"Like what?" Bob said.

"Like hands, feet, legs, arms, a torso, and a head," Nina answered. "All surgically removed from six different corpses."

CHAPTER THREE

7:30 P.M.
THE ABANDONED GOLDSTADT MANSION
ANOTHER DARK AND STORMY NIGHT

"Hurry, Fritz! Hurry," the scientist called up to his assistant.

"Yes, Master," Fritz yelled down from the loft. He secured the last link in the chain that extended from the loft to the floor some fifty feet below.

"We can't miss tonight's storm!" the scientist insisted. "We may never have another chance at this!"

"Yes, Master!" Fritz yelled back. He landed flat-footed on the hardwood floor and, pulling the chain with him, scampered to the scientist, who was standing beside a gurney. He attached the length of chain to one corner of the table. "All four chains are secured, Master."

"Very good, Fritz. You have done well, my friend."

Fritz giggled — a deep, menacing sound.

"Get over to the wheel and await my signal."

"Yes, Master." Fritz waddled to a big, metal wheel attached to one wall of the large room.

Herr Henry Frankenstein worked hurriedly. The

sky had darkened an hour earlier. Distant lightning and thunder spoke to him of the coming storm. Last night, his plans had been thwarted by the police officer who had invaded his warehouse. But then Fritz had found the secluded Goldstadt Mansion, the perfect spot for Herr Frankenstein to work in security and anonymity.

Anonymity, he thought. He ran his hands over the muslin wrapping in which he had swathed his creation. *Anonymity? Not for long. No, the world will soon know of the greatness and majesty of my creation.*

Herr Frankenstein attached a wire to an electrical patch on the neck of his creation.

The lightning and thunder were distant no longer. A fiery white light sliced through the black sky. The thunder began as a slow rumble and crescendoed into a staccato tympani.

Startled, Fritz jerked his face to the opening high in the loft. The four chains seemed to disappear into the blackness of the sky. He knew that the chains were attached to pulleys and the pulleys were attached to a wooden rigging he himself had built. From the pulleys, the chains joined as one, like four roads meeting, and through the end link of each chain ran a steel cable that ran up to a large pulley in the center of the rigging. The cable continued until it was diverted downward by another pulley, finally ending at the massive wheel Fritz now held in his hands.

He had the most important job. His master had told him so. And his master never lied to him. Ever.

Fritz frowned. Images flashed through his fuzzy brain like out-of-focus images on a movie screen. He didn't understand what had happened, and his sleepy mind never thought to ask why it had happened. But over the past few days the out-of-focus past had tried to break through his foggy brain. He had nightmares. Nightmares of a monster that his master had created. Nightmares that this monster had killed him and then hung him from a ceiling rafter.

Fritz shuddered. That's all they were. Nightmares. Nothing else. The master told him they were only nightmares. And the master never lied to him. Ever.

The lightning exploded in strands of white fury and the thunder clapped like an angry god slapping the face of the sky.

Fritz jerked his face once more to the opening in the loft fifty feet over his head. He pointed to the darkness with a short, stubby finger. "Master! Master! The storm! The storm!"

"Yes, Fritz," Herr Frankenstein replied. He kept his eyes on his fingers, and he kept his fingers busy attaching the final electrical wires to the body that lay before him.

This time. This time. They will see. They will regret what they have done to me. They will pay for their insults and their abuse.

He wouldn't make the same mistake this time. He had learned from his past mistakes. That, he thought, was the stroke of true genius. To try and then fail and then learn. He couldn't live in the past. He wouldn't live in the past. The past wasn't real.

Herr Frankenstein sighed, straightened up, and stepped back.

"Finished, Fritz." He looked at his creation. Electrical wires protruding from beneath the cloth attached to the decaying skin of the body he had built from six different corpses.

For four months, ever since he and Fritz had awakened in this brave new world of color with senses he had never before experienced, Herr Frankenstein and his deformed assistant had prepared for this moment, the moment in which the name of Frankenstein would bring awe and inspiration to the huddled masses.

To the sons; to the House of Frankenstein! a distant voice echoed through his head.

Four months of research and sifting through mortuaries for the perfect body parts for his masterpiece. Four months of digging up the graves of the recently departed. Before, in the days of grays and blacks and whites, he had made the mistake of taking the bodies of criminals and the poor. This time, he was more selective.

The head had come from a boy who the newspapers had described as a Tom Cruise look-alike, with a boyish and rugged dark look. The torso was taken from a high school weight lifter who had achieved much fame as one of the strongest teenagers in the country. The arms had belonged to a teen who claimed to be the pull-up champion in a nearby high school. The legs were from a cross-country champion. The feet were taken from a promising young dancer. And the hands had come from the star football receiver who held the state record for number of catches in one season.

He had wanted the hands of the detective who had intruded upon him the previous night, but other police officers had arrived, and Herr Frankenstein and Fritz had barely escaped with the hands they had already harvested.

But the *coup de grâce* was the brain. The brain that Fritz had stolen from the university's School of Medicine. The brain had belonged to the state high school chess champion.

All his corpses had been cut down in the prime of life. All had died within the last four months. He had had to do some repairing of the decaying skin from each corpse, but overall, he was proud of his work. This creature would not be insane like his previous creation. This being would live to bring him fame and fortune — and to bring revenge on those who had mocked his theory of regeneration.

He threw his head back and laughed. As though in response, the sky lit up with fire and rolling thunder. Herr Frankenstein rubbed his hands on his bloodstained lab coat.

"Now, Fritz!" the scientist yelled. "Now!"

Fritz smiled, his yellow, rotten teeth grinding as he pulled on the wheel. The chain slowly began to move, and the table upon which the muslin-swathed monster lay inched its way toward the darkness at the top of the loft.

In the old days, primitive vacuum tube instruments that sparked and hissed and buzzed had confined him. In this new age into which he had been reborn, he found that sand had been transformed into silicon and the silicon transformed into wonderful omnipotent machines.

Herr Frankenstein watched as the table disappeared into the dark sky. He tapped the ENTER key on his computer keyboard. The computer's hard drive hummed and whirred to life. Binary code in a green digital hue raced across the computer screen. It increased in speed until the numbers and the lines were a blur.

An arc of electricity snapped and crackled, and then struck the lifeless body upon the gurney.

The scientist continued to enter commands into the computer, sending electrical impulses to the dead flesh of the stitched monster. These impulses carried more than energy into the dead tissue of the body. This was the true genius of the scientist who sat at the keyboard.

He had learned his lesson. This time he would not only implant the spark of energy into his creation, he would imbue it with the spark of humanity. The binary codes racing from the computer to the Creature's flesh carried the computerized DNA code of *Homo sapiens*.

Lightning illuminated the darkness at the top of the loft. The fiery fingers reached across the sky and massaged the still form on the gurney. Smoke rose from the muslin wrappings. The gurney and the monster were lit in a ghostly white glow.

The irony was not lost on the scientist. It wasn't angels Herr Frankenstein was creating. It was life. Human life. He would once more be like a god when his Creature walked upon the unsuspecting Earth.

CHAPTER FOUR

SAME TIME
SCHOOL OF MEDICINE, UNIVERSITY OF MIAMI
EXTENSION CAMPUS
SAME DARK AND STORMY NIGHT

"His condition's been upgraded from serious to guarded, so we've moved him into a private room. At the rate he's progressing, he might be out in a couple of days." The doctor scanned the chart and then looked at the three teenagers standing before him. A young male as big as a house, a female who would be a knockout in a few years, and a short, stocky male with dishwater hair that looked as though it had never been introduced to a comb. "If you promise me you'll only stay a few minutes, I'll let you see him."

"We promise," Nina said.

"Okay," the doctor said. "Besides, he's been asking for you three." He looked at his watch. "Fifteen minutes. That's all." He shoved his pen into his pocket, and walked away.

"Pretty cool that Detective Turner asked for us," Bob said.

"Well," Joe said, "he doesn't have any family here, and I'm sure he knew we would show up when we heard he was hurt."

"By the way," Nina said as they headed toward Detective Turner's room, "what play are the freshmen doing this year?"

Bob just groaned in response.

"What play, Joe?"

"*Julius Caesar*. I'm stage manager," Joe announced proudly.

Nina frowned. "Don't tell me you're Brutus," she said to Bob.

"No," Bob said through clenched teeth.

"Who?" Nina asked Joe.

"All Hail Caesar," Joe said.

"That ought to help your ego," Nina said. "You know Caesar's biggest problem? Not listening to his wife. If he had listened to his wife, he wouldn't have been assassinated."

"Oh, right," Bob said. "It's great. I get killed in the third act and I'm out of the play."

"You get to appear as a ghost in the fifth act," Joe said.

"Really? Cool." Bob swaggered down the hallway. "I shall be remembered as the best ghost to graduate from Ponce de Leon High."

"Of course," Nina said, "that's based on the assumption that you're going to graduate from high school. At the rate you're going, I'd be surprised to see you last past Christmas break."

"And what part, pray tell, did you have in your freshman class play?" Bob asked, one eyebrow cocked. Nina was two years older than Bob and Joe — a junior. And in Bob's opinion, she gave herself far too many airs about it.

"I played one of the three weird sisters in *Macbeth*," Nina answered.

"Typecasting?" Bob inquired with a smile.

Nina was about to give a scathing reply when Joe suddenly said, "Here's his room."

"We'll settle this later," Nina growled at Bob.

"Don't make promises you can't keep."

The School of Medicine was an extension campus of the University of Miami. It had taken over the ailing San Tomas Inlet Hospital several years earlier, turning the nearly defunct hospital into a top-notch care facility.

Detective Turner's room was cool and dark. An IV of saline solution ran into his right arm. A brace around his neck kept his head still and erect, so his bony chin jutted out. His face was covered in a dark shadow.

"Hello, kids," he said, his voice a gravelly whisper.

"Hey, Detective Turner," Captain Bob said. He removed his hat and stuck it in his back pocket.

"Hey," Nina said. "How are you?"

"I'll never play the violin again."

"You never played it to begin with," Joe said.

Turner smiled. "How are you doing in school, Bob?"

Bob shrugged. "Got to dissect a frog today. That's about the coolest thing we've done. I like anatomy. I'm thinking about going to medical school."

"The only way you'll get into med school," Nina said, "is as a volunteer subject."

Bob ignored Nina and pulled up a chair next to his mentor. "Nina said they found six bodies in the warehouse."

"Six corpses that had been stolen from the cemetery," Turner added.

"Any idea why?" Nina said.

"I have a vague idea." He looked at the three teens. "And I have a feeling I know what each of you is thinking."

They were all silent for several moments.

Then Bob said, "You still don't believe us, do you? We fought Dracula and the Wolf Man. Now dismembered corpses are found in a warehouse and a brain's stolen from the School of Medicine. I'm not too good at the new math, but I say it all adds up to Dr. Frankenstein."

Detective Turner nodded. "Could you hand me that hospital mug, please?"

"Sure," Nina replied. She grabbed the big mug and brought it to Turner's lips. For the first time, she could really see the extent of the detective's injuries. His lips were puffy and blue from bruising and his left eye was swollen shut. Ugly blue bruises sat on both cheeks, and a bump the size of a golf ball protruded from his forehead.

"Not a pretty sight, am I?" Turner said, smiling wryly.

"You weren't all that good-looking to begin with," Joe said, grinning.

Nina tilted the plastic straw to Turner's lips and the detective drank slowly.

"Well?" Bob said. "You know, this isn't just a social meeting here. Dr. Frankenstein has dug up six corpses, hacked them up, and stolen a brain. I say it's time to head for the hills because Frankenstein has created another monster!"

"I believe you," Turner said. "Thank you," he said to Nina.

"You're welcome." She set the mug on the table.

"What?" Bob said, puzzled.

"I believe you," Turner repeated.

"You do? Why?"

"You can't leave well enough alone, can you, Bob?" Nina asked, frowning.

"All right, I admit that with the other two monsters I thought you three were crazy." He laughed dryly. "This is the twenty-first century, and you three want me to believe that monsters from seventy-year-old movies have come to life in our peaceful little village."

"Seventy years ago," Bob said, "space travel was science fiction. Now we're placing robots on Mars."

"Yeah. You're right. I guess that's one reason I believe you." Turner swallowed. "That and the six corpses we found. Plus, I saw them."

"You saw who?" Joe said.

"I saw Frankenstein and his assistant at the warehouse. You think I got this way by tripping over my own two feet?"

"I don't mean to sound rude," Bob said, "but why didn't they kill you?"

"I had turned on my radio to call for help. I didn't get a chance to send a message before the hunchback attacked me, but the radio still sent out a signal. When I didn't respond to the dispatcher's query, they sent the cavalry to my rescue. Good thing, too. The last thing I remember was Frankenstein saying something about taking my hands."

"How do you know he was Dr. Frankenstein?" Nina said.

"You three think you're the only ones who watch old horror movies? I grew up on that stuff. I used to have all the models: the Frankenstein monster, Dracula, Werewolf, all of them. That was Frankenstein I saw last night. And Fritz, his assistant. And, by the way, it's not Doctor Frankenstein. It's Herr Frankenstein. He was only a student in the movie."

"He's right," Bob said.

"Did they look like the characters in the movie?" Joe said.

"Frankenstein looked like himself. Fritz was changed somewhat. His face was roughly the same, but he had long, massive arms, bright red hair that shot out in all directions, and large yellow teeth that looked as though they were about to rot right out of his head. He had the hunchback like in the movie, but his legs were short and stubby. Like a monkey."

"Strange," Nina said, her brow furrowed. "But it fits. In each case so far, the monsters have had some similarities with their movie images but have somehow managed to alter some things about themselves so we can't recognize them right away."

"You know," Bob said professorially, "most people believe that Igor is Herr Frankenstein's assistant. Igor didn't come around until the sequels. Fritz was the original assistant but was killed by the monster in the original *Frankenstein*."

"Now, that's weird," Nina said.

"You ought to know weird, sister," Bob said with a smile.

Nina rolled her eyes. "What's weird is that Fritz is with Herr Frankenstein now, but in the movie he's killed about halfway through."

"Yeah," Joe added. "In one scene he's teasing the monster with a torch, and then in the next, he's swinging from a rafter. You know who put him there — the monster."

"Okay," Nina said. "So like with the Wolf Man, we not only have one character to deal with, we have two: the scientist and his assistant."

"Three," Bob said. "The Creature as well. You can bet that Frankenstein is making another Creature as we speak."

"With Dracula and the Wolf Man, we were dealing with monsters that relied on full moons and physical transformations," Joe said. "Frankenstein is different."

"How do you figure?" Turner said.

"He's an egotistical madman," Joe replied. "In the movie, he thinks he has discovered the secret of creation, and when the Creature he has created turns out to be imperfect, he tries to destroy it. The Creature reacts as any child would — he strikes out."

"So are we fighting Frankenstein or his monster?" Bob said.

"I'd say we've got both to deal with," Joe responded. "But it'd be nice to catch up with Frankenstein before he completes his creation."

"Good plan. Okay," Nina said. "We learned with Dracula that the monster will look for something familiar in this world that reminds him of his movie world. Dracula found the Carfax Hotel and my friend Angela, who looked like his long-lost love. The Wolf Man and his mother found an Ocala Indian who was a shapeshifter and lived in Wales. In the movie, Herr Frankenstein was in Germany. So what is there around San Tomas that would be familiar to Herr Frankenstein and Fritz?"

All were silent for several minutes. The room hummed as the vital-statistics monitor recorded Detective Turner's breathing, heart rate, and blood pressure.

Then the room was filled with a brilliant light. A

second later, a thunderous explosion rattled the windows of the hospital room.

Bob looked at Joe. Joe looked at Nina. Nina looked at both of them.

"This time of year," Nina said, "we have the most awesome storms in the country. Storms that produce a thousand lightning strikes a night. More lightning strikes than any other place in the country. Just what a mad scientist needs if he wants to bring dead flesh back to life."

"Hey-ho, boys and girls," Captain Bob said, putting on his yacht captain's hat. "Looks like it's time to raise a little hell."

CHAPTER FIVE
TUESDAY EVENING
HOME OF FRANCISCO TREJO

Trey tossed his books on the old desk and then threw himself onto his bed. He put his arms behind his head and stared at the dull white ceiling. He had a lot of work to do — both homework and housework. His aunt and uncle were both at work, as was his older sister. He would be alone for several more hours. When he had lived in Cuba, he and his family had a small, cramped apartment, and he'd dreamed of a time when he would have space to himself, to be alone. He never realized just how lonely being alone really was.

Trey sighed, pushed himself up off the bed, and started for the kitchen. He would start dinner and then clean the living room. His older sister would be the first one home. She had a job after school, just a few hours a week, but it brought in some extra money for the family. Then his aunt and uncle would come home around eight P.M. They all would sit down to dinner. His uncle would ask him and his sister how they had done in school. After dinner, Trey and his sister would clear the table and do the dishes, and then they would each go to their rooms to do their homework.

They had been in America for only three months, and those three months had been the hardest of Trey's young life. He never complained, though. Although they lived in a run-down rental in a poorer section of San Tomas Inlet, and they all had to work hard to make ends meet, what little they had in America was much better than the little they'd had in Cuba. At least in America, Trey did not have to worry about the police coming in the middle of the night to take his opinionated uncle away.

Trey turned on the stove burner and placed a pot of water on top of the flame. Rice and beans was a staple in the Trejo home. Sometimes they had some beef, but mostly they ate boiled chicken. Every night at the dinner table, Trey's uncle would say that someday, if they all worked hard, they would live in a big house and eat like a rich family.

"Good things come to those who wait," his uncle always said, "and work hard while they are waiting. The best things in life are those for which we work the hardest."

Trey thought his uncle a little old-fashioned at times, but he would never say so out loud. Respect for family was paramount in his culture, from grandparent on down to grandchild.

Trey stirred the rice to keep it from sticking to

the bottom and sides of the pan. He smiled to himself. He liked the boy he had met in biology class — Capitan Bob. Trey wasn't sure why he was called Capitan Bob. Perhaps he belonged to some student military club, just as Trey had belonged to the Young Pioneers in his Cuban school.

Whatever the reason, Trey liked Bob. He was funny and smart. They had finished dissecting and labeling their frog long before anyone else in the class and the teacher had praised them. In the three months he had been in America, Trey had learned that American teenagers were often rude and disingenuous when it came to their teachers and their schools. In Cuba, students, parents, and society held teachers in utmost respect.

Capitan Bob seemed to be well liked because the other students were often laughing at what he had to say. Except for a tall, thin girl named Megan. For some reason, Megan disliked Capitan Bob, and said rude things to Trey's new friend.

Trey set the table and then headed to the living room, a dust rag in one hand. At least this would be the last time Trey would have to clean the house by himself. His uncle had given him permission to work after school a couple of days during the week. Trey had gone to the guidance counselor's office that morning to look at the help wanted list. He'd found a job at a small restaurant on the beach, gone for an interview after school, and been hired on the spot.

Trey bent over to wipe the dust from the coffee

table. A sharp, stabbing pain fired through his head like a spike. He hit the floor on his knees and grabbed the sides of his head. He tried to scream, but only harsh gurgles came from his throat. He fell to his side. He could feel his heart beating against the sides of his head like a hammer striking concrete.

The seizure would last for a minute or so. They had begun a year ago. The doctors in Cuba had no explanation.

Trey never remembered the seizures. He would wake up, wondering how and why he had fallen asleep. He would be confused, disoriented. Sometimes, during the seizure, he would bite his tongue and the sticky taste of blood would be in his mouth. Afterwards he would sleep for hours or he would hop right up as though nothing had happened.

Occasionally, Trey would have nightmares in the moments that the seizure lasted. Sometimes these nightmares were of fantastic beasts from ancient myths, and sometimes they were simply full of shouts and screams in the deep darkness of his subconscious.

Tonight, however, the nightmare was all too real. He was lying on an operating table in a dirty hospital room. A hunchbacked ape hovered over him with a scalpel in one hand. A voice somewhere in the darkness spoke in deep tones that echoed throughout the room.

"It is perfect," the voice said. *"His brain is perfect."*

The hunchbacked ape moved to the top of Trey's head, brandishing the scalpel with a menacing leer. Through the thickness of the hellish nightmare, Trey tried to scream, but when he opened his mouth all that came out was a fountain of blood and gore.

CHAPTER SIX
TUESDAY, 10:30 P.M.
OVER AT THE FRANKENSTEIN PLACE

"Bring it down, Fritz! Bring it down!" Herr Frankenstein stopped his mad pecking on the keyboard. On the opposite side of the room, his hunchbacked henchman was spinning the large metal wheel.

The gurney slowly descended from the loft that opened onto the stormy night sky. Smoke rose from the muslin swathing in which the cadaver rested.

Despite the coolness of the evening and the wind that whipped down from the loft, sweat poured from Herr Frankenstein's brow. He flipped the last switch and the electrical humming of the machine slowly died away.

An eerie silence fell over the room. Herr Frankenstein looked at the still form on the gurney. He stepped toward it.

Fritz joined him. The hunchback's eyes were wild with anticipation. Fritz slowly edged a finger to a spot where the muslin had burned away from the body.

Catching the movement out of the corner of his eye, Herr Frankenstein slapped the hunchback's hand away. Fritz hissed as he rubbed his sore hand.

"I will not make the same mistake as last time," Frankenstein said, his eyes gleaming. "This time, my Creature will live to make fools of those who dared to laugh at me!" He grabbed a stethoscope from a table behind him. He listened intently, moving the stethoscope around the sternum. A smile came to his lips. "A faint heartbeat, Fritz. Quickly, we've got to unwrap him and prepare him for the injection."

"Yes, Master," Fritz replied eagerly.

Herr Frankenstein grabbed a pair of scissors and began cutting the muslin wrapping away from his creation. "From death, I have created life. Life!" The scissors cut away strand after strand. "Fritz, no longer will humans be confined to a few decades of life. From this point on, people can live as long as they desire. This body has been infused with the fire of life, and with my nondegenerative formula, it will not deteriorate, but become strong and impervious to disease."

"Yes, Master," Fritz responded.

The doctor had exposed the entire upper body. He checked the joints at the shoulders and hands — no stitches. Only smooth skin, as though all the parts had been formed from the same embryonic cells. He checked the sutures that attached the head and neck to the torso. Again, only smooth skin. The scientist smiled. He placed the edge of the scissors under the muslin along the left jaw line and began to cut.

From life comes death comes life comes death. . . .

Frankenstein started as he saw a thin line of red blood appear from under the muslin, near the Creature's mouth. He hurriedly cut the rest of the muslin and removed the bandages.

The mouth of the monster was open slightly. The tip of his tongue poked out between his lips and teeth. The tongue was black, and it was bleeding where the monster had bitten down.

"Quick, Fritz, a sponge." The scientist opened the mouth slightly and the tongue disappeared back into the Creature's mouth. Fritz handed a surgical sponge to his master. The scientist sopped up the blood from around the monster's lips. He looked into the face of his creation. No heavy brow, no protruding electrode bolts, no flat head. He touched the Creature's forehead. It was warm — flesh and blood. The greenish skin that days before was a mush of decaying flesh was now pulled taut over the skull beneath it. The Creature was beautiful.

"Do you know what this means, Fritz?" The scientist held up a swab covered in blood. "Do you?" His voice was nearly hysterical. "He's bleeding. Do you understand what that means?"

"What, Master?" Fritz asked innocently.

"Dead men don't bleed!" The scientist threw his head back and laughed. "He's alive! He's alive!"

The Creature's fingers moved slowly, and one hand slowly lifted from the gurney.

"Look, Fritz! Look!"

Frankenstein leaned over the gurney, eyes wide, a demented smile stretching across his face.

The Creature moaned.

"Quick, Fritz, the straps, the wires," the scientist ordered.

Fritz quickly pulled the attached wires from the now-living skin of the Creature. Then he unbuckled the straps that ran across the Creature's chest and legs.

"Now, help him slowly from the gurney, Fritz."

They pulled the legs around, and Fritz pushed up from the shoulders.

"He's heavy, Master," Fritz said, groaning.

Frankenstein steadied his creation as Fritz moved him into a sitting position.

Frankenstein took a penlight from his pocket and pointed it at the closed eyes of his creation. He gently lifted one eyelid and then the other. He smiled as he watched the pupils dilate in reaction to the light. The eyes opened and stared blankly forward, a dull white film covering whatever life was behind them.

Frankenstein lifted the chin of his creation. The face was perfect — it could adorn the cover of a teen magazine. He checked the hairline. The dark hair hid the slight scar where he had cut away the skull to put in the perfect brain of the chess champion.

He suddenly clapped his hands. The Creature jerked. His hearing worked.

"Now," Frankenstein said. "It's time. Help me, Fritz."

"Yes, Master."

The scientist and the hunchback stood on either side of the Creature and grabbed an arm. They pulled the Creature from the table, and the monster stood on his own.

"He's tall, Master," Fritz said as he craned his neck to look up at the Creature.

The Creature swayed on uncertain legs. Even hunched over, he stood 6'5". He straightened himself and stretched to his full height — seven feet. He breathed deeply, his chest expanding in and out. Taut muscles stretched on bones. His broad, round shoulders rose with each breath. His skin had a greenish but pleasing hue. As if a light had been turned on behind them, the Creature's eyes suddenly shone with life.

"Move back, Fritz. Let him stand on his own. He must learn to stand on his own."

Frankenstein and Fritz moved back from the monster. The monster swayed. Fritz moved to catch him.

"No!" Frankenstein shouted. "He must learn on his own."

The Creature leaned forward. His right leg shot out and he stepped forward. Then the left leg followed.

"He's walking, Fritz. He remembers." Frankenstein's face was aglow.

The Creature continued walking, jerking each leg forward, his arms out in front of him to steady his gait. With each lurch, the Creature gained more confidence and began to take longer and quicker steps. A cautious smile of triumph spread across his face.

"This time, Fritz, I will show those fools what life really is," Frankenstein said, his eyes glazed over in euphoric wonder. He was in front of his creation, walking slowly backward, his hands up and motioning the Creature to continue.

The scientist bumped against the table upon which the computer sat. He moved around it, but the Creature was so transfixed on moving forward that he didn't notice. The Creature's massive leg hit the table and it tilted over. The Creature looked down and watched in horrified puzzlement as the table fell over, the computer spilling from its surface.

The monster screamed as the sparks from the monitor flew into his face. He tried batting away the onslaught of fire. The monster backed up, swinging his giant arms in the air.

Herr Frankenstein stepped toward the monster,

his arms in front of him. "It's okay. It's gone away," he said, desperation in his voice.

"It's okay," Fritz echoed. He reached out and touched the smooth skin of the monster's back.

Startled, the monster turned, his arms still flailing. One arm caught Fritz across the neck. Fritz slammed into the ground, his hands around his injured throat. He struggled to breathe, each breath a wheezing, high-pitched rasping.

"No!" Frankenstein yelled. He stepped toward his creation.

The monster turned, fire and fear in his eyes. He swung at his creator. Frankenstein ducked.

"He's mad!" Frankenstein yelled. "He's insane!"

The Creature stepped forward. Frankenstein grabbed the keyboard and swung it at the monster. The monster caught it and crushed it in the palm of his large hand. Then the monster reached out and grabbed the scientist by the collar, lifting the man off the floor until they were eye to eye.

Herr Henry Frankenstein stared into the dark eyes of his creation. Dead eyes. The eyes — the window to the soul. But there was no soul in this — this *monster*, and Frankenstein knew it. He had made the same mistake. He had given his monster strength, agility, finesse, quickness, and brains, but he had forgotten once again about the human soul.

"Put me down," Frankenstein ordered. "Put me down, you beast."

The fear on the monster's face was swept away by pain and confusion. His eyes misted over. He did not understand what had happened. A low whine came from deep within his throat.

"Put me down!" Frankenstein demanded.

The monster lowered the scientist to the floor.

Frankenstein stepped back. Disgust covered his face as he stared at the monster he had created. "I'll have to destroy you like I did once before. I'll have to start over. And next time, I'll write a program for the human soul."

The mist cleared from the monster's eyes and he looked at his creator, who had an ugly, dangerous look on his face. A distant memory poked through the fog of his brain, and he was caught up in a sudden force of fear and terror. The monster screamed and swung out at his creator.

Frankenstein caught the full force of a broad palm along the side of his face. He fell to the ground, the deep, dark blanket of unconscious enfolding him.

The monster looked about him. The other creatures did not move. Somewhere in the fog of his reawakened brain, he knew that what he had just done was not good. He knew that he would be punished for harming the other two creatures and breaking the machine.

Lightning flashed and the roar of thunder cascaded down into the room. The monster cowered, raising his hands in a useless effort to thwart off the brilliant light. When the light and the noise vanished, the monster straightened himself and growled at the sky.

A moan from below brought his attention back to the floor. The smaller creature, the one holding his neck, was moving.

The monster knew he must escape his punishment. Into his primitive, misty memory came images of chains and the deep pain of loneliness. The monster staggered from the room and out into the cold, wet rain.

CHAPTER SEVEN
ABOUT THE SAME TIME
NINA NOBRIEGA'S CONVERTIBLE

"One good thing about fighting this monster," Nina remarked as she guided the car out of the School of Medicine parking lot and onto Beachfront Road.

"What?" Bob said from the backseat.

"We won't have to put up with your stinky old wolfsbane."

"I've got some left," Bob said with assurance.

"But it won't work on Frankenstein. There's no wolfsbane involved in the movie. Wolfsbane only worked on the Wolf Man."

"She's right," Joe added.

"Great," Bob said.

"I wonder how the camera will work this time," Joe said. "With the Wolf Man, we had to use a bit of magic and modern technology. Who knows what we'll need this time around."

Lightning jetted across the sky. Heavy drops of rain hit Nina's windshield. She flipped on the wipers.

"Need to get this baby home and into the garage," Nina said.

"Me first," Bob said.

"There's got to be more than just the lightning that would attract Frankenstein to San Tomas," Joe said. "But what?"

"Maybe you ought to watch the movie when you get home," Nina suggested.

"Yeah. That's a good idea," Joe said. "Be kind of freaky watching it without the three main characters."

"You know," Bob said, sitting up. "Why haven't we ever watched any of those movies all the way through? Maybe we could find a clue to stop the others from appearing."

Nina turned the car onto Sea Lane and nosed it through the gates of the San Tomas Inlet Mobile Park. "That's not a bad idea, Bob. But it's too late tonight. We need to save that project for a weekend. I've got a chem exam tomorrow, and I'll bet you haven't even done your homework."

"What homework?" Bob said with a smile.

"I rest my case," Nina said, shaking her head.

"Well, I'm going to watch *Frankenstein* tonight," Joe said. "I've already done my homework."

"Show-off," Bob said.

Nina stopped the car. "Here you go, madman."

Joe opened his door and leaned forward. Bob squeezed through the small opening between the seat and the door frame.

"You know," Bob said, grunting as he crawled out, "if you'd let me ride up front, I could get out a lot easier." Nina never let him sit in the front, and it really got on his nerves.

"If I let you ride up front," Joe said, "Nina would be in such hysterics after one mile that we'd get in a wreck and all be killed."

Bob popped out of the car and fell to his knees. He stood, brushed the mud from his jeans and adjusted his hat. "I'm off, said the madman."

"Later, man," Joe replied, shutting the door.

His friends drove away. Bob watched for a few seconds, letting the heavy, cold raindrops hit him. He turned his face to the sky. He wondered if his mother would let this count as his shower. It was getting late and he wanted to spend some quality time on the computer. It had been days since he had visited his favorite Web site, and he wanted to check out any new weird stories that had been posted in the interim.

He turned and trotted to his front door. He was especially proud that the site had posted his stories about Dracula and the Wolf Man. Of course, if Joe or Nina were to read his accounts, they might have a slightly different recollection of Bob's role in saving the day. But he knew his friends weren't fans of the site and was assured that his hero status would remain intact.

The mobile home was dark as he entered. His mother was the manager of the Beach Burger, so she had to close the restaurant each night. Perhaps she would close early tonight. Bob was a little worried about his mother being caught out in the storm.

The mobile home shook as thunder detonated in the night sky. Nina was right: San Tomas Inlet had some of the most beautiful and deadly electrical storms in the nation.

Bob went straight to his room, stepping over the clothes that cluttered his carpet. The only light was the warm and familiar glow from the computer monitor sitting on his desk. He patted the top of the monitor. "Did you miss me?"

He clicked on the Internet icon and waited as he listened to the modem dial up his ISP. He wished his mother could afford DSL.

His favorite site popped up as soon as the modem connected. He was happy to read the reviews of his stories, all favorable, especially one from somebody named Goliath. Goliath said he loved the story, that it was well written, and that Bob must be some kind of hero to single-handedly fight off both Dracula and the Wolf Man.

Bob cocked one eyebrow. "Of course I am."

His e-mail chimed. Bob waited as his messages downloaded. He hadn't checked his mail in days. There was a lot of spam, some messages from Joe from two days earlier, and an e-mail from Dr. James.

Bob sat up. That was cool. Dr. James had sent him

an e-mail. Normally, a high school student would be a little worried if a teacher sent him an e-mail, but biology was the only class in which Bob actually did his work. It was also the only class he was passing. During the first term, Bob had almost failed botany, but Dr. James had given him some extra help, and Bob had begun to think of the older man more as a mentor and not just a teacher.

FROM: bioteach@poncehighsantomas.edu
TO: madman@santomasnet.com
SUBJECT: Anatomical Experiments

Hey, Captain Bob,

I'm working on some anatomical experiments after school and was wondering if you would be interested in helping out. You don't need the extra credit — this time — but I thought you'd have fun and maybe even learn something. Anyway, I could use your help. If you're interested, meet me in the lab after school tomorrow.

Dr. T. J.

Captain Bob smiled. He suddenly felt important: *I could use your help.* Well, if Dr. T. J. needed his help, then he would gladly give it. Besides, although he may not need the extra credit now, he probably would in the future. The way Bob looked at it, he was investing in his future grades.

He clicked on REPLY and sent a message saying he would like to help, but that he couldn't stay any later than 4:30 as he had to work at the Beach Burger on Wednesday nights.

He hit SEND and the message disappeared.

Captain Bob leaned back in his chair, his hands behind his head. He wondered what kind of anatomical experiments Dr. James was working on. The frog dissection earlier that day had been pretty cool. Trey hadn't hogged all the good cutting. Bob had heard that advanced students got to work on larger animals.

The trailer shook again, but no thunder had exploded this time. Bob bolted upright. A loud pounding reverberated throughout the trailer. Bob leaned over his computer desk, pulled the curtains apart, and peered out the window. Distant lightning flashed and silhouetted clouds miles away. Bob squinted his eyes through the thick rain and heavy darkness.

The pounding resounded again, and the trailer shook. Then Bob heard a yowl. He turned from the window, ran to the front door, and stepped out onto the wooden deck. The cold rain sent a chill through his body. Maybe it was just kids playing a prank. But then the pounding started again. It was coming from the back of the trailer.

Bob darted back inside, down the hallway, and threw open the back door.

"Hey!" he shouted. "If I catch you kids, I'm gonna —"

A body flew past Bob. Stunned at the sight, Bob just stood for a moment, squinting his eyes, wondering if he had really just seen a body fly past. The dim yellow security light of the trailer park was of little help.

Then, amid the thud of the heavy raindrops, he heard a low growl. Not the growl of a dog or a cougar. A human growl. Bob slowly turned his head to the right. Although he was standing on the top step of the back stoop, his eyes were level with the deep, dark eyes of the intruder. Bob saw a large, thick object headed toward him. Instinctively, he ducked. He heard a crash and then a splintering. When he looked up, he saw it was an arm — an arm that was now embedded in the outside wall of his mobile home.

Bob leaped to his left and onto the mushy, wet ground. He stumbled forward and tripped, sliding several yards on the waterlogged grass.

Lying near him was a body — the body over which he had just tripped, the body that had flown past him moments earlier. At first, Bob thought it was a human, but in the dull light he could now see that it was the dead form of an Old English sheepdog that belonged to a woman who lived several trailers from Bob.

Bob started toward the dog, but stopped as a dark shadow fell over him.

The giant madman had pulled his arm out of the wall. He was lurching toward the dead dog. He stood over it, his large hands clenched into sledgehammer fists. In the dim yellow of the trailer park's security light, Bob could see the large bared teeth, the maddening scowl. He was like a wild animal protecting its kill.

Lightning flashed, and Bob could now see the giant clearly. He was stunned to see a teenager's face attached to the giant body.

Attached? That's no giant madman, Bob thought. *That's the monster! That's the creation of Herr Frankenstein!*

Captain Bob turned and fled off into the cold, wet night.

CHAPTER EIGHT
THE TREJO HOME

"He is okay," Trey's sister, Gloria, said, wiping her brother's forehead with a wet cloth. "I think he will sleep the rest of the night."

"I will move him to his bed," his uncle said. The large man bent over and easily lifted his nephew from the couch and took him into his bedroom. He placed Trey on the bed, and Gloria covered her brother with an afghan. They both left the room quietly.

Gloria walked into the kitchen. "I will help you, Tía Maria," she said to her aunt, who was scrubbing the burnt rice from the pan.

Her aunt smiled and said, "I will telephone your parents in the morning and tell them about Francisco's seizure. They should know."

"I hope they will be able to come to us soon," Gloria said as she dried the dishes.

"I know you miss them, but they did what they thought was best. They will be in America sooner than you think. You must do your homework now.

I will finish up in here. Go now," she said with a smile.

Gloria kissed her aunt on the cheek and went to her bedroom. She sat at her desk and opened her American history book. She tried to read her assignment and answer the questions, but her mind darted from her brother's seizure to her parents still in Cuba to the students at her new school. Gloria was a senior at Ponce de Leon High. Some of the students treated her nicely. Others treated her like a disease. Cuban teenagers were no better. They had cliques and social outcasts and misfits just like in America. The difference was that in Cuba, social standing was based on your parents' standing in the Communist Party, while in America, social standing was based on how much money your parents had. The kids at Ponce de Leon High who treated Gloria like a disease did so because her family was not rich. The vast majority of the students at Ponce High knew little to nothing about political subjects.

Gloria gave up and closed her book. She turned off her desk light and stared out the window. Rain was falling from the black clouds that hung low in the sky.

Gloria was about to turn away and get ready for bed when a shadow crossed her window. She leaned forward and squinted her eyes to focus on the shape moving through the heavy rain, then gasped when she saw a giant man lumbering through the back alley. He was carrying something in his arms. The giant moved into the yellow circle of the security light.

Gloria's eyes widened. The giant was indeed a man; rather, a giant man with a teenager's face, and in the giant's arms was the limp body of a large dog, his long white-and-gray fur matted by rain and blood.

CHAPTER NINE
7:30 A.M.
WEDNESDAY
PONCE DE LEON HIGH SCHOOL CAFETERIA

"You've got to stop calling after midnight," Joe said as they sat at the cafeteria table. He scooped up a spoonful of lukewarm oatmeal and pushed it into his mouth. His eyes were a little bloodshot and puffy. "My mom's ticked. She's going to take the phone from my room if you do it again. You woke up my sister, too."

"What was I supposed to do, wait until morning? I had to talk to someone. Detective Turner isn't any help, and I can't call Nina: She'd kill me. Turn the ringer down on your phone."

"Just don't call after midnight."

"Oh, I'm just supposed to let the Frankenstein monster kill me."

"He wasn't after you. He just happened to be in your neighborhood."

"That's not a comforting thought."

"How long are you going to stay at your uncle's beach house?"

"Until Mom feels it's safe to return to the trailer

park. I told her and the police that a man had killed Mrs. Smith's sheepdog. The hole in the back of the trailer looks like someone shot a two-by-four through it."

"They didn't find any evidence of where the monster went?"

"No. It started to rain again and by the time the police got there, all the tracks were gone." Bob played with his hard, stale toast, thumping it on the plastic tray. "I think this toast is left over from 1973." He tossed the toast on the tray. It landed with a thud. "They could use it to rebrick the school."

"They could use this stuff they call oatmeal as mortar," Joe said with a smile.

Bob chuckled. "I don't mind staying at Uncle Bruce's house. It's a regular bachelor pad. The problem is, Mom's there, so it's really not like a bachelor pad."

"Yeah, like you have a lot of prospects for using a bachelor pad," Joe said.

Bob ignored the slight. "I'm going to the hospital after school to talk to Detective Turner. Now that he believes us about the other monsters, maybe he'll believe that I saw Frankenstein's monster."

"It didn't look anything like the movie monster?"

"No." Bob thought for a moment. "Remember that kid that died a few months back, saving that baby from the fire? He kinda looked like him."

"Yeah, I remember that. But I can't think of his

name." Joe sat up. "You know, we need to find out about the bodies that were dug up. Detective Turner can get us the names."

"What names?" Nina asked, joining them at the table.

"The names of the bodies that Detective Turner found at the warehouse," Joe said. "Might be a pattern."

"The first one was stolen just over four months ago," Nina said, "just after Count Dracula appeared."

"It seems that Herr Frankenstein has been around for a while, working on his Creature," Joe said.

"It seems that he's succeeded," Bob added. "The Creature attacked me last night."

"Last night?" Nina asked in disbelief. She listened intently as Bob told his story. When he'd finished, she turned to Joe. "Did you find anything in the movie?"

"No. Nothing out of the ordinary, except that Herr Frankenstein, Fritz, and the Creature were gone," Joe replied.

"Okay. I've got to stay after school and talk with Mrs. Hoving about the exhibition coming next month," Nina said as the first bell rang. "I shouldn't be any later than four. But I want to see Detective Turner, too. So let's meet in the parking lot, all right?" Nina didn't wait for answer. She stood, straightened her books in her arms, and walked away.

"You know," Bob said, "I still think letting her in the Forensics Club was a bad idea. She's so bossy."

"Hey," Joe said, standing, "you're the one who said we needed the dues."

"I was right," Bob said as he and Joe headed out of the cafeteria. "But I wasn't counting on her being so cheap. She still hasn't paid up."

"Yes she has," Joe said.

"When? I'm the treasurer."

"Not anymore," Joe said. "She made herself treasurer, and now we have $5.35 in our club account."

"When did this happen? I didn't know about any meeting."

Joe smiled. "There wasn't a meeting." He furrowed his brow. "I think they call it a *coup*."

"Oh, brother. Just what we need: Adolf Nobriega running the Forensics Club."

"*Ja volt!*" Joe said with a laugh.

3:45 P.M.
DR. JAMES'S BIOLOGY CLASSROOM

"That's good. That's good," Dr. James said. "Now ease up, pull it around, and tie it off."

Captain Bob's tongue stuck out of the corner of his mouth as he concentrated on pulling the suture through the skin. Sweat beaded on his forehead. He had gone through the procedure twice before and each time he had botched it. The procedure looked simple when Dr. James had demonstrated it to him an hour earlier.

Bob shook his head to get the sweat out of his eyes. Now he understood why doctors had nurses patting their foreheads. A doctor can't just reach up and dry himself, not when he's got his hands in the middle of somebody's guts or lungs.

Bob looped the surgical silk and then passed the end through the loop. He gently tugged with the suture clamps and a small, nearly invisible white knot formed.

"Very good, Captain Bob," Dr. James said. "That's as good as a second-year med student."

"Thanks, Doc," Bob said, a big smile on his face. Then he yawned unexpectedly. "Man, I didn't know I was so tired."

"Surgery does that to you," Dr. James said. "A doctor spends twelve, sixteen hours in the operating room without realizing how much time has passed because he's so busy concentrating on doing his job. Afterwards — he's exhausted."

"All I did was reattach the frog's leg to the torso. Three stitches. And I'm pooped. You made it look simple."

"That's because you channeled all of your energy into doing your job. It's the same with anyone who really cares about his work." He looked at his watch. "You need a ride to work?"

"No. I've got my moped."

"Little chilly out." Dr. James looked out the window. "Gonna be another storm tonight."

"I'll be okay," Bob said as he threw on his leather jacket. "This baby keeps me warm. We've been through a lot together."

"What's that written on the back?"

Bob turned.

"Born to Raze Hell! Pretty clever. You think of that?"

"Joe and I did. Last summer."

They walked out of the classroom and out of the school building toward the parking lot.

"Why didn't you become a doctor?" Bob said.

"I am a doctor," Dr. James said with a smile.

"I mean a medical doctor."

"I am a medical doctor. Even practiced for a while. But I enjoy the philosophy of medicine more than the actual practice of it. I decided to concentrate on research and teaching. I enjoy teaching. Besides, someone's got to teach the next generation of doctors, right?"

"Never thought of it that way," Bob said, straddling his moped. He stomped on the foot crank and the moped sputtered to life.

"Before you go, Captain Bob . . ."

"Yes, Dr. James?"

"How are you getting along with your new lab partner?"

"Trey is cool. He's smart, but he's not bossy, you know? I think I'll keep him."

Dr. James smiled. "That's nice to know, Captain Bob. I just didn't want you running him off before he's had a chance to adjust to his new school. He's only been in America about four months."

"Really?"

"You didn't know?" Dr. James adjusted his glasses. "Francisco Trejo and his sister escaped from Cuba last summer. They're staying with their aunt and uncle until their parents can leave Cuba. The boat they were on almost sunk. They were saved by a Canadian fishing boat that brought them to Florida."

"Wow. I remember reading about that now. I didn't know that was Trey."

"Once immigration cleared them, they came to San Tomas to live with relatives. I tell you this just so you know what Trey went through to get here. So you can keep your fake barf and flattened plastic bug guts to yourself. Let him get adjusted to living a normal American life before you expose him to its, let's say, more wild side."

"Sure. Will do," Bob said with a salute. "See you tomorrow."

Bob puttered away on his two-cycle moped, trying to steady the small bike in the strong wind that blew off the ocean. He had liked Trey since meeting him the day before, but now he seemed more like some kind of hero.

Captain Bob had wanted to visit Detective Turner with Joe and Nina, but at lunch he remembered that he had to work at the Beach Burger. He still had forty dollars to go on paying Megan McMahan back for her singed weave. Bob sighed, twisted the accelerator on the moped, and sputtered down Beachfront Road to work.

"Hey, Hubert," he said ten minutes later, entering the restaurant.

Hubert looked at his watch. "You're late."

"Traffic." Bob stepped behind the counter, hung up his leather jacket, and put on his Beach Burger shirt and ball cap.

"There's no traffic this time of year," Hubert replied, frowning.

"Yeah, I know." Bob walked over to the deep-fat fryer and shook a basket of fries sitting in the boiling grease. "Where's Mom?"

"Went home. Said you were to lock up."

Bob grimaced. He hated locking up. That meant taking out the trash, sweeping and mopping the floors, and shutting off all the lights. The Beach Burger closed early on Wednesdays, but he still wouldn't get out of there until eleven P.M. He wished he had brought his books with him so he could have worked on his homework, give his teachers a thrill.

"She also said you were supposed to train the new guy," Hubert said. He was sweeping the floor.

"What new guy?" Bob said with a frown.

"Me," said a voice from the walk-in freezer. It was Trey, carrying a box of frozen burger patties.

"Trey!" Bob exclaimed. "Cool. When did you get hired?"

"Yesterday afternoon. I saw the advertisement on the work board at school."

"You didn't tell me in class."

"I didn't know you worked here. Your mother is the manager?"

"Yeah. Cool, huh?"

Hubert scooped the dirt and wadded papers into the dustpan. "Your mom says you better train him right or else."

"Hey, I trained you," Bob said.

"Yeah," Hubert said. "That's why your mom wants you to do the job right this time."

Bob frowned. "Great, Hubert. Don't you think you better take those fries out now?"

Hubert just glared at him.

"So, what's it like living in Cuba, Trey?"

"I do not wish to speak about it," Trey said. He took several frozen hamburger patties from the box and threw them on the grill. They sizzled and the ice quickly turned to steam.

"That bad, huh?"

"No, it is just I do not like to talk about the past. I left many friends in Cuba and did not get a chance to say good-bye to them. How long do I keep the meat on the grill?"

"Here, I'll show you." Bob moved behind the

counter, grabbed a spatula, and pressed down on the patties. They sizzled and hissed, and then he turned them over.

"Hey, where'd you get that bump?" Bob said. He hadn't noticed it in school.

"I tripped and fell," Trey said, putting his hand on the small bump that protruded from his left temple.

"I guess brains and coordination don't necessarily go hand in hand," Bob said with a smile.

"No, I guess not."

"How come you speak English so good?"

"Well."

"Huh?"

"Well. You should say, 'How come you speak English so well?' not 'good.'"

"Uh, yeah," Bob said, trying not to look embarrassed. "How come?"

"I have had English lessons for seven years. But we learn the British way of speaking."

"Like what?"

Trey flipped a couple of burgers. "For example, when we were at the immigration office, my uncle would ask where the lift was and no one could understand him. Then a man from England overheard him and explained that Americans call a lift an elevator."

"Cool."

"And Americans want to put ice in everything. My teeth hurt from so much ice."

"Well, in America," Bob said, putting the finishing touches on an order, "you can have things any way you want them."

"Still, some people laugh. Some of the other students make fun of my accent."

"They're jealous," Bob said. "They're short on brains and long on stupidity. Order up," he called out. Hubert shuffled to the counter, grabbed the two orders of burgers and fries, and shuffled away. "I rest my case," Bob said, nodding toward Hubert. Trey suppressed a laugh and threw two more frozen patties on the hot grill.

The night went by quickly as Bob showed Trey his duties. Because it was the off-season, they weren't that busy.

Trey had brought his books, and since he and Bob had some of the same classes together, they worked on homework when the restaurant was empty.

"I'm still surprised you know English so well," Bob said. "This is my second year of Spanish, and I can't get past *'Hola. Comó está usted?'*" Except when Bob said it, it came out *"Holey. Comma estes you said?"*

Trey laughed at Bob's mispronunciation. "Russian used to be taught in our schools, but now English is the language of choice for the Comsomols."

"The what?"

"In our Communist schools, children start out as

Young Pioneers. You have seen them on television wearing the white shirts with the red bandannas."

"Yes," Bob said. "I just thought it was the Boy Scouts or something."

"No, that is the official school uniform. A Young Pioneer takes examinations and becomes a Comsomol, someone who one day might be a leader in the party."

"Were you a Comsomol?"

"Yes. I am not ashamed to say so. It is — I mean, was — our way of life. I did not agree with all that our government did, but I could not attend university unless I was a Comsomol."

"That's cool," Bob said, scribbling an algebraic equation. "We do what we have to do."

"I'm glad you do not try to shame me," Trey said. Bob looked up. The Cuban boy's eyes were shining. "I have been called some bad names by some of the American students. One cannot help where one is born."

Bob chuckled. "Don't worry about it. We have some real yahoos in this country. I get called names all the time."

"And it does not bother you?"

"Sure, it does: shrimp, mop head, trailer trash."

"What do you do?"

"I put bugs in their food."

Trey laughed. "I would not want you for an enemy, Capitan Bob Hardin."

"Neither would I, *amiga*," Bob said.

Trey laughed again. "It's *amigo*. *Amiga* is for a friend who is a girl."

Bob sighed. "Sorry. I have a hard enough time with English."

"I will help with your Spanish and your English and your algebra and your biology and you will train me to be the number-one hamburger cooker in Florida." He stuck out his hand.

Bob grabbed it. "It's a deal, *amigo!*" Bob looked at the clock. "Man, it's time to close already. Let's clean up and *vámonos!*"

"Groovy, home boy," Trey said, standing.

"Uh," Bob began, "we really don't say 'groovy' anymore, and 'home boy' went out around the same time as Hammer."

"Okeydokey, pokey."

Bob laughed and handed Trey a broom.

Half an hour later, they were walking down the boardwalk.

"I do not think I have ever seen an all-night dental clinic," Trey said as they passed the Night Emergency Dental Clinic.

Bob shuddered and walked a little faster, remembering the dentist who'd turned out to be Dracula. "Believe me, you don't want those guys working on you. They can be a real pain in the neck."

"I thought they worked on teeth."

"How are you getting home?"

"My sister is to meet me at the road."

"I have my moped. I'd give you a ride, but it barely runs with me on it, and I don't have an extra helmet."

"You have a motorcycle? Groovy."

"Do me a favor. Stop saying groovy. Deal?" Bob said.

"Okay, homey," Trey responded.

They stopped beside Bob's bike. "Yep," Bob said, looking at the battered red-and-silver machine with pride. "This baby will get fifty miles a gallon. Of course, it only holds a half gallon at a time."

Trey smiled. "I still do not understand gallons and feet and miles and inches. In Cuba, we have the metric system."

"So does the rest of the world," Bob said. "Everyone but America. We're still using the king's measurements." He looked around. "Your sister's late. Want me to wait?"

"No. I do not mind being lonely."

"Alone."

"Pardon."

"You don't mind being alone."

"That is correct."

Bob smiled. "Okay. I'll see you in school tomorrow. Thanks for helping me with the homework."

"Groovy," Trey said.

Bob straddled the moped and kicked the engine. It sputtered to life. "We've got to get you a more updated slang dictionary. Later."

"*Adiós,*" Trey said with a wave.

Bob slowly pulled away. He had gone only a block when he looked in his cracked rearview mirror. He still hadn't replaced it since the time he crashed his moped on the beach, when giant ticks had attacked him months earlier.

Trey stood under the light on the sidewalk alongside Beachfront Road. Bob glanced up and then back down at his cracked mirror. Trey was gone. *That was quick*, Bob thought. Then he saw Trey run into the beam of the yellow streetlight. A short apelike creature followed. The creature grabbed Trey and threw him to the ground.

Bob turned the moped around, twisting the accelerator as hard as he could.

Trey lay still on the ground. The apelike creature hovered over the still body, sniffing it. It looked up as Bob drew closer, the moped's small headlight hitting the creature full in the face.

Bob was not frightened at encountering the grizzled, twisted face, the yellow, rotten teeth, and the large hump of the hunchback Fritz, just as Detective Turner had described him. But he was surprised to find Frankenstein's assistant attacking Trey.

Bob aimed his bike at the hunchback. Fritz did not move. The hunchback's frown turned up slowly into a hideous smile.

Just as he reached Fritz and Trey, Bob swerved his bike to the side and leaped at the hunchback. He hit Fritz in the chest and bounced off like a rubber ball against a concrete wall. Bob landed on the ground with a thud, the wind knocked out of him.

Fritz waddled over to Bob and stood over the boy, cocking his head from side to side in curiosity.

Bob caught his breath and kicked out. He had aimed his kick for Fritz's throat and expected to connect with soft flesh. Instead, his foot hit hard plastic. Searing pain ran from Bob's foot up his leg and into the small of his back. He cried out. Fritz laughed. He grabbed Bob's leg and lifted the teen from the ground, holding him upside down.

"Master does not want you," Fritz said, his voice soft as gravel. "He wants the smart one. You are not smart."

Bob twisted, trying to break the steel grip of the ape-man.

"You are not the smart one. You are the foolish one. Fritz is hungry. Fritz has not eaten because he has waited for the smart one. Master will not mind if Ol' Fritz eats now. He will not mind if I eat you."

Bob watched in horror as Fritz opened his mouth and aimed the yellow, rotten teeth at the fleshy center of Bob's thigh.

CHAPTER TEN

A burst of light. A screech of tires. A pounding of heavy, quick feet on asphalt.

Fritz dropped Bob and disappeared from sight.

Bob hit the ground. Although stunned, he was quickly on his feet.

Joe stood next to him. "You okay?"

"Yeah," Bob said, holding his sides and gasping for air. "I thought I was dead meat."

Fritz had rolled several yards away. Now the apelike man stood on his feet, crouched over, his knuckles dragging on the ground.

"Master wants the smart one," Fritz said.

"What's he talking about?" Joe said.

"I don't know. He said the same thing and then started to chomp on me."

"Master will *have* the smart one." Fritz rushed at the two teens, his arms spread out. Each arm caught a teen, and before they could react, both were thrown to the ground.

Fritz turned to Trey, who still lay unconscious.

"Oh, no you don't, you big ape," Nina said. She tossed her humanities book at his head.

Fritz tried to duck, but the book caught the corner of his head, twisting it around. He screamed as the neck brace kept his neck from moving with it. He growled at Nina, turned, and ran off into the dark.

Joe stood. "That was easy."

"Too easy," Bob added.

Nina knelt beside Trey. She turned him over. A reddish bump had popped out on the right side of his forehead.

"Is he okay?" Bob said, kneeling next to Nina.

"He's unconscious."

"What is happening?" came a frightened voice from behind them.

They turned to see a teenage girl approaching them. "Francisco," she said as she knelt beside the boy. "He is my brother," she explained. "What has happened?"

"He was attacked," Bob said.

"Help me carry him to the car, please," the girl said. Joe grabbed Trey's feet while Bob lifted his friend by the shoulders.

"I will take him home," the girl said.

She opened the door and they laid him in the backseat. The girl helped guide Trey into the backseat, and Bob brushed up against her arm. A shudder ran through him.

"You are his friends?" the girl asked.

Bob straightened up and looked at her. She was as tall as he was, with long dark hair and thick eyebrows. Her skin was smooth and her face was clear. When she spoke, she had a slight lisp as well as a Cuban accent like Trey's. The words seemed to roll off her lips like a cool breeze on a hot day.

"Y-yes," Bob said with a stammer. "I'll make a statement to the police."

"No," the girl said quickly, fright in her voice. "No police." She hopped into the car and started the engine.

"But —" Bob began.

"Please, do not be angry," the girl said. She sped away.

"What was that all about?" Joe asked.

"In Cuba, the police take people away in the middle of the night. Everyone's scared of them," said Nina.

"No wonder she doesn't want us to call them," Joe replied.

Captain Bob said nothing. He was looking after the car as it disappeared into the night, his eyes wide and glazed over, his mouth slightly open.

"Hey," Nina said, snapping her fingers in front of Bob's face. "Earth to Captain Bob. Put your eyeballs back in your head."

"Who was that?" Bob said, his voice soft and distant.

Nina spoke quickly. "Her name's Gloria, and she's Trey's sister. She's in my humanities class.

She's a senior, a straight-A student, and doesn't have time for freshmen boys. Especially since Oscar Morales is always hanging around her."

Bob shook his head. "Just my luck."

"What happened?" Joe said. "Bob! What happened?"

"I don't know," Bob replied. "I was riding away when I saw Fritz attack Trey. All that creep said was that the master wanted the smart one."

"What does that mean?" Joe said.

"I don't know."

"Maybe we ought to go after Fritz," Nina said.

Bob looked off in the distance. "He's disappeared." Bob took a step and then limped. "Man, he's got a grip."

"Was he going to bite you?" Nina said.

"He said something about the master wanting the smart one and then said he was hungry and started to gnaw on my thigh." Bob rubbed his sore thigh. "I don't think he broke the skin before you tackled him. Thanks," Bob said, turning to Joe.

"No problem," Joe said.

"Oh, man!" Bob spotted his moped. It had crashed into a ditch on the opposite side of the road.

Bob hobbled over. "Oh, *man!*" The front wheel was bent and the engine was covered with water. "Well, that's the end of that."

"I'm sorry, Bob," Nina said, placing her hand on his shoulder. "I know that bike meant a lot to you."

"Oh, man," Bob said softly. "It was my freedom."

"I know," Nina said. "I feel the same about my car. At least you're okay."

"And so is Trey," Joe added.

Bob smiled, but it was a bittersweet smile. Trey was safe, bruised but safe. But Bob's bike was beyond repair. He had bought it with the money he had earned working at Universal Studios Florida the past summer, and now it was bent and waterlogged and ruined.

"C'mon, Captain Bob," Nina said, her hand still on his shoulder. "Let's get you home. We'll come back tomorrow and give it a decent burial."

Bob did not move.

"C'mon, buddy," Joe said. "We've got something to tell you about Herr Frankenstein. Something that Detective Turner discovered today."

Bob sighed. He turned, walked over to the curb, picked up his captain's hat, and put it on his head. "This is personal now." He walked to Nina's car and hopped in the back without any argument.

Nina looked at Joe, who only shrugged.

CHAPTER ELEVEN

THURSDAY, 12:30 A.M.
AN OLD SHED ON THE OUTSKIRTS OF SAN TOMAS

The Creature shivered in the cold. His skin felt cold and clammy. He moaned, and tears welled in his eyes.

A glint of a full moon peeked out from behind the dark clouds that covered the sky. The water from the sky had stopped falling. He had fought with the heavy drops as they fell until he realized that he could not stop the water from assailing him. He had found shelter in a small shack. Shelter from the cold water that fell from the sky, but no shelter from the bitter cold he felt within him.

His memory jogged back to the night before, when he had awakened and taken his first steps. The look on his creator's face had given him hope and joy and confidence. And then his creator had looked at him with horror and disgust and called him a monster, a beast that had to be destroyed.

The words echoed through his reeling brain like a gunshot. The Creature put his hands to his head and pressed, trying to stop the cruel words from ricocheting around his mind.

He had wanted to kill his creator. He had swung out and hit him, and then the creator lay still. He was about to crush his creator's skull when the sky bellowed and threw fire at him. Then he had run from his place of birth.

He had stumbled out into the dark, wet night, looking for something — he didn't know what. The night continued to howl at him, but he growled back and the noise and the fire went away.

Then he found the dog in the wet night. He walked up to the dog, his hands out, palms up. He didn't want to scare it, just to be its friend. But he could smell something coming from the dog, something primitive and alarming. Fear.

A sudden fury gripped him and he grabbed the dog. He lifted it from the ground and shook it. The dog growled and whimpered and bit him about the arms. He was not evil. He was not a monster. He was a human being, more than a human being. Why couldn't the dog understand that? Why couldn't his creator understand that? He shook the dog harder, trying to make it understand. But the dog only cried out in pain and bit at the monster.

The monster screamed, too, but his screams were the screams of frustration and abandonment. The Creature could not form the sounds to make the words that were flooding his sick mind. He shook the dog like a baby shakes its rattle.

Soon the dog stopped squirming. The monster stopped shaking it. The dog was still. The dog would not run away anymore. The dog was like him now. Alone. And dead.

The monster sat in his small, dilapidated shed with the dead dog lying next to him. The dog's face was turned upward, its blank eyes open, staring into infinite night.

The monster picked at his arm and pulled a swatch of skin from it. He felt no pain as he stared down at the blackened muscle that rested beneath it. He had a heart and it beat, but the blood that his heart sent pulsing through his body was the blood of the dead.

Out of instinct, the creature knew what the creator would do next. He knew that the creator would want to kill him. The Creature wasn't going to let that happen. The Creature would stop his creator, even if it meant killing the man who had given him life.

The monster glanced over at his new friend and petted the dog as though they were lifelong friends.

CHAPTER TWELVE

SAME TIME
UNCLE BRUCE'S BEACHFRONT HOUSE

"It's not all that impossible," Nina was saying. She took a drink of hot chocolate.

"I'm not saying it is," Bob replied. "I'm just not willing to jump to conclusions."

"That's a first," Nina retorted.

"Not so loud; you'll wake Mom," Bob warned.

Bob, Nina, and Joe sat around the small table in the kitchen of the small beach house.

"Detective Turner thinks we ought to concentrate on finding the Creature that attacked the trailer park and forget about Herr Frankenstein. He's not the problem," Joe said.

"Fritz is a problem," Bob said, rubbing his thigh.

"Fritz is a patsy doing whatever his master tells him to do," Nina said. "He's got about as much willpower as those toads you dissected yesterday."

"If this were the movie, we could just wait for the Creature to try to kill Herr Frankenstein," Bob said.

"Well, this isn't the movie," Nina replied with a frown.

Bob glowered. "It's a good thing this isn't a movie. We'd need a wide-angle lens just to get that fat head of yours in the shot."

Nina smiled back. "Yeah? Well, we'd need to do an extreme close-up just to be able to find your brain."

"Kids, kids," Joe said softly, tapping a finger on the table. "You need to tuck your egos in for the night. We have a bigger problem than who can out-smart the other."

Nina sighed. She looked at Bob. She could tell he was tired. The bags under his eyes were like two puffy half moons. She didn't know why, but Bob just seemed to crawl under her skin sometimes, like an itch you can't scratch.

"What do you think Fritz meant about 'the smart one'?" Nina asked him.

"I don't know, but he was after Trey. And Trey is pretty smart," Bob said. He stared at a spot on the table in front of him, his vision blurring.

"But how would Herr Frankenstein know that? Besides, he doesn't kill people," Joe said. "He only digs them up after they're dead. The Frankenstein monster makes them dead."

Bob sighed. Then he yawned. "You're right. But it was Fritz trying to kidnap Trey. And then he tried to take a bite out of my leg. All the Creature tried to do was protect his dead pet. I say we have to find Herr Frankenstein and Fritz."

Low thunder rumbled in the distance.

"Tomorrow," Nina said. "Right now, we've got to get some sleep. As odd as this may sound, we not only have to find a mad scientist, his hunchback cannibal, and a murdering man-made monster, but we've still got school tomorrow."

"Man, I wish it were the weekend," Bob said.

They all stood.

"How are you guys on absences?" Joe asked.

"What are you thinking?" Nina responded as they walked outside into the wet night air.

"I've only got one," Joe replied. "That means I can have two more absences before it begins to affect my grades. I can spare one day to look for Herr Frankenstein."

"I've got three already," Bob said. "But I'm willing to chance it."

"You don't have many chances left," Nina said. "Your grades are terrible. One more absence means you'll automatically be on probation next semester."

"She's right," Joe said. "Besides, it's probably best that only one of us do some snooping around. More subtle that way."

"I've got a chem exam," Nina said. "If I miss it, I have to take one of Mr. Cravens's famous makeup exams, and they're twice as hard as the regular exam."

"Okay," Joe said. "I'll tell my mom I don't feel well and then when she goes to work, I'll do some snooping around town. I'll meet you guys at the Beach Burger right before Bob's shift. Okay?"

Bob and Nina nodded. Then Nina and Joe hopped into her convertible and drove off.

Bob looked up into the ominous clouds of the dark night. He wondered what Fritz had meant about the master wanting the smart one. And he thought about his faithful moped.

A single drop of rain hit him in the eye. "Ow!" he muttered, rubbing it. Even nature was against him.

CHAPTER THIRTEEN
THURSDAY, 12:30 P.M.
LUNCHROOM, PONCE DE LEON HIGH

"How are you feeling, Trey?" Bob said as he joined Trey at a cafeteria table.

"I am well. Thank you," Trey replied. The swelling on his temple had gone down overnight and only a small bruise remained on his right cheek.

"Do you remember what happened?" Bob said.

"No. My sister said I fell and hit my head on the curb." He looked at Bob. "That is not unusual." He looked away as he said it, avoiding Bob's eyes.

"Guess all the excitement of learning to make fast food was more than you could handle," Bob said with a smile.

"She said you helped me. Thank you," Trey said.

"That's what friends are for," Bob replied.

"Yes. Thank you," came a soft voice from behind Bob.

Bob turned. Gloria slid into the chair next to him.

Bob tipped his yacht captain's cap and stuttered, "M-my pleasure."

"Trey says that you are a capitan," Gloria said.

"A what?"

"I'm sorry," Gloria said with a smile. "A captain."

"No," Bob replied, blushing. "I just like to be called captain." He lifted his hat. "My uncle gave it to me. It's a yacht captain's cap."

"I see." Gloria shifted in her seat. "My uncle says he is grateful that you helped Francisco last night. He is worried now. He wants Francisco and me to quit our jobs and come home right after school."

"Why?" Bob asked.

"Because I was attacked," Trey said. "My uncle treats me like I am a child."

"Francisco!" Gloria said harshly. She turned to Bob. "Also, he wants you to know that Francisco has seizures."

"Gloria!"

"It is nothing to be ashamed about, Francisco." Gloria turned to Bob. "*Tío* Miguel says he wants you to know because you are his friend and are in many classes together. If Francisco has a seizure, *Tío* Miguel knows that you will help him."

"I don't know what to say," Bob said. But he felt proud that Gloria trusted him to help his new friend.

The bell rang, and the other students headed out of the cafeteria slowly, as though they could prolong the inevitable return to classes.

Gloria stood. "Thank you, Capitan Bob." She picked up her books and joined the throng.

Bob stared after Gloria. Then he turned around and found himself face-to-face with Oscar Morales.

"Don't you have someplace else to be?" Bob said, annoyed.

"I stand where I want, freshman. That means you either move or get run over."

"I've had better offers," Bob shot back.

"Let go of him, Oscar," Trey demanded.

"You stay out of this, *pobrecito*," Oscar growled at Trey. Then he turned back to Bob. "Yesterday you get me in trouble with that scary English teacher. Today I see you with my girl. Do you have some kind of death wish?"

Bob paused. There were two conflicting voices in his head — the voice of reason, which sounded a lot like Joe's voice and his own gut instinct, which was urging him to let Oscar have it.

"Well?" Oscar said.

Bob couldn't resist. "The only wish I have," he began, "is that they find a cure for that disease of yours."

"Oh yeah? What disease is that, smart guy?" Oscar said sarcastically.

"La enfermedad estúpida."

Oscar's eyes flared. But before he could act, Bob dropped his backpack on the big senior's foot. Oscar howled in pain, clutching his toes.

Bob took advantage of the moment to grab his backpack and get out of there. *At least I've finally found a good use for those books*, Bob thought as he sped down the hallway.

"Capitan Bob! Wait!" It was Trey.

"Sorry I had to eat and run," Bob said as his friend caught up with him.

"No, it is I who am sorry. Oscar is very protective of my sister," Trey answered. He looked embarrassed. "He is an old friend of our family."

"Don't worry about it," said Bob. "Let's get to class. We're going to be late."

They headed up the stairwell toward English class.

"You know what the chiropractor said to the good-looking blond who had arthritis in her elbow?" Bob asked Trey as they entered the classroom.

"No," Trey said.

"What's a bad joint like this doing in a nice girl like you?"

"What kind of arthritis was it?" Trey asked as they sat down.

"Never mind," Bob replied. "I think the joke got lost in the translation."

"Did the doctor cure her arthritis?" Trey said, a puzzled look on his face.

Bob sighed deeply and opened his copy of *Julius Caesar*.

The period passed quickly. Bob tried to concentrate on his role as Caesar, but he kept thinking about Joe and what he was doing. Bob kept breaking character, forgetting his lines, and Ms. Bashara was not long on patience. Bob became more frustrated as they rehearsed the assassination scene from Act III at least a dozen times. Ms. Bashara smiled each time Bob, as Caesar, was stabbed again and again.

But Bob still managed to get under Ms. Bashara's skin. He refused to take off his yacht captain's hat, claiming that it gave him inspiration. If that weren't enough, after each onslaught of stabbings, when Brutus thrust his knife into his friend Julius Caesar, Bob would utter something other than the famous *Et tu, Brute*. One time it would be "Eat toes, Brutay." Another it would be "Screw you, Brutay." But the one that really drove Ms. Bashara wild was when Captain Bob blurted out, "Ouch, ouch, ouch, ouch" with each stab wound.

Finally, Ms. Bashara threw up her hands and told everyone to take off their togas and return to their seats.

Bob did so with a smile.

CHAPTER FOURTEEN

1 P.M.
SOMEWHERE IN SAN TOMAS INLET

The blister on Joe's right heel was the size of a quarter. He limped as he walked, trying not to think about it. He asked himself more than once why he had let his mother talk him into getting such uncomfortable tennis shoes. He couldn't wait until warmer weather, when he could slip on his sandals every day. At least they went with the myriad Hawaiian shirts he had in his closet.

Joe had started his search just after his mother had left for work at 8:30 that morning. First he went to the library and read up on all the bodies that had been stolen. He was hoping he would find some clue, anything, a pattern in names or dates or types of deaths, but he had run up against one brick wall after another. He made a list of the names, dates, deaths, diseases, hair color, eye color, occupations, and even nationalities — anything he could glean from the obituaries or biographies of the six dead people stolen from their graves. The only one he recognized was the college sophomore who had died while saving a child from a fire earlier that year. Joe hadn't known him, but the story had been on all the local news stations.

Then the idea came to him that perhaps all six were special in some way, maybe prodigies in some field of endeavor. But this, too, was a dead end.

When his research at the library and county records office proved fruitless, Joe began to walk around town. He didn't know when the blister had begun to form, he just knew that suddenly it was there, and it was large and sore, and he had not accomplished anything. Joe decided to go home, take care of his blister, and pretend to have sufficiently recovered from his "illness" by the time his mother returned home to go meet Nina and Bob at the Beach Burger.

Joe hailed a cab, and in a short while, he was home.

Joe dressed the blister and put on a pair of comfortable old tennis shoes. He was about to settle on the couch and watch some TV when he heard the garage door open. He glanced at his watch — 2:15. His mother was home early from work. He plopped onto the couch and tried to look both well and a little ill.

He waited. His mother didn't come in. Joe sat up. Maybe she had groceries. No matter how sick he was pretending to be, he wasn't going to let his mother carry in the groceries by herself.

Joe walked into the kitchen, opening the door

that led into the garage. It stood dark and empty. A perplexed look crossed his face. He had distinctly heard the garage door open. Joe flipped up the light switch, but the garage remained dark. Joe flipped the switch again. The light was out.

Joe went back into the kitchen, reached into the pantry, and pulled out a lightbulb. He turned back to the door.

Fritz was standing there, his shock of red hair in sharp contrast to the dark garage that framed him.

Joe started to back up, but one of the hunchback's strong arms grabbed him. Fritz tried to drag Joe into the garage, but the freshman was too strong. Joe jerked away, but in doing so, fell to the floor. Fritz pounced on him.

Joe grabbed the neck brace and pulled on it as hard as he could. Fritz screamed and fell to the side. Joe sprang to his feet, but he wasn't quick enough. Fritz got him by the shirt and yanked him back.

Joe turned and landed a roundhouse right on Fritz's left cheek. The hunchback's face twisted in pain, but he kept his grip on Joe. Joe took another swing, but Fritz grasped his fist and squeezed as hard as he could.

Blood seeped out between the hunchback's fingers. Joe felt his head begin to swim. The hunchback laughed.

Fritz jerked his arm, and Joe fell, landing on his

back. Fritz put his knee on Joe's chest and pushed down, forcing the air out of Joe's lungs.

"Ol' Fritz is the strongest, yes," Fritz said, a toothy grin on his face. "Ol' Fritz will bring back the big one for Master. The big one and the smart one for Master. Master wants them both."

Darkness began at the outer edges of Joe's eyes and slowly rippled inward. He no longer felt his hand in the steel grip of the hunchback. He tried to suck in air, but the pressure on his chest was so great that he could only manage meager breaths. They weren't enough.

Soon the darkness had washed over him, and Joe fell into a chasm of endless nightmares.

CHAPTER FIFTEEN
3:05 P.M.
DR. JAMES'S BIOLOGY CLASSROOM

"They're playing my song!" Bob cried as the last bell of the school day rang. He jumped up from his seat and headed to the door, pushing through the mob of students jostling one another as they headed out to freedom.

"Captain Bob!" Dr. James yelled from the front of the room.

Bob had reached the doorway and turned around. "Whoa!" he said as he was pushed into the hallway. He had to catch himself to keep from falling backward. "Watch where you're going!"

"Don't stop in the middle of the doorway," Megan said testily. "This isn't a bus stop, you know."

Bob stood. "You know, Megan, I bet you're the kind of girl that guys take to the movies when they want to see the picture."

Megan's eyes flared. "What are you saying?"

"I don't chew my popcorn twice," Bob said, grinning, then stalked back into the biology room.

"You really ought to be nicer to Megan," Dr. James said, his hands in the pockets of his stained old lab coat. "It's not really polite, not to mention fair."

"I know," Bob said, sighing with mock remorse. "I could beat Megan in a battle of wits with one brain tied behind my back."

"That's what I want to talk to you about, Captain Bob." Dr. James returned to his desk and lifted up a sheet of paper. "I checked your grades and your file. Anybody looking at your intelligence test scores and your grades would think you had a split personality. While your IQ has been rated at 130, your grade point average is one-point-nine, a D plus."

Bob flushed. If anybody else had pointed this out to him, he would have told him to mind his own business. But Dr. James wasn't just anybody. He had overlooked Bob's clowning and pranks and offered him extra help when other teachers had just recorded Bob's poor marks in their grade books.

Bob knew he deserved the reputation he had earned and he also knew that the teachers had tolerated his outbursts and laziness as much as they could. After all, teachers are human, too. Even if just barely.

"If you want to get into a premed program like we talked about, you'll have to do better than this. Medical school requires that you have straight A's, good attendance, and recommendations from your teachers." Dr. James dropped the paper on his desk.

"The first half of your freshman year is almost up, but it's not too late. We can't do anything about your first-semester grades; however, we can start working on bringing up next semester's."

"How can I get into medical school if my GPA isn't what it should be?" Bob asked, sitting at a lab table.

"I've got some pull at some of the universities," Dr. James said with a smile. "Some of the instructors in those schools were once my pupils. And I'll let you in on a little secret." He sat on the edge of his desk. "I've had my share of Captain Bobs in my day, and they're all practicing medicine now."

"Really?" Bob asked.

"But they had to work hard. So will you." Dr. James stood. "And we can begin tomorrow after school."

"Yeah, I can do that." Bob stood. He looked at his watch. "I've got to get to work."

"Okay," Dr. James said, extending his hand.

Bob just stood there for a moment. He had never shaken a teacher's hand before. He always imagined that a teacher's skin was as slick as a frog's back. Bob grabbed Dr. James's palm. "Thanks."

"Now go to your job and be ready to work hard tomorrow. You're going to be working with another student I've been tutoring after school, a senior by the name of Oscar Morales. Do you know him?" Dr. James asked.

"I've run into him a couple of times," Bob replied, grimacing.

"Good. Oscar may not look like it, but he's got a sharp mind and a good head for research."

"I'll bet."

Dr. James smiled, "Now, Captain Bob, how do you feel when people judge you before they know you?"

Bob sighed. He couldn't argue with Dr. James.

"Oscar's got a keen interest in anatomy. In fact, I haven't had to teach him much at all. It's almost as though he was born with surgical knowledge."

Bob perked up. "What?"

"He's a natural for surgery. You'll learn a lot from him. You've got the brains to succeed." Dr. James tapped Bob on the forehead. "But you must have the heart to succeed." He tapped Captain Bob on the chest.

Bob walked out of Ponce High in a daze. He had to walk to work because of his wrecked moped, and this gave him time to think. He was excited about studying with Dr. James, but he couldn't believe he was going to have to work closely with that brutish lout Oscar Morales.

Then Dr. James' words broke through his reverie: *You've got the brains. You must have the heart.*

Bob had never heard those words from a teacher before. All he ever got was lectures and fortune-cookie solutions.

The brains. The heart.
The brains!

Bob stopped in his tracks. *Of course! The brain!*

Herr Frankenstein had created another monster. He had used body parts from different corpses. He had stitched them together and somehow brought life to the dead tissue. Just as in the movie.

And just like the movie, when Fritz stole the brain, the most important component of Herr Frankenstein's monster, he must have stolen the wrong one. He had taken a defective brain.

Bob quickened his pace. He huffed and puffed as he walked. He was really out of shape. The peanut-butter-and-bologna sandwich and Twinkies he had had for lunch rested in his stomach like a bowling ball. Every now and then the bruise Fritz had left on his thigh would pulse, sending a sharp pain through his leg.

Finally, he made it to the Beach Burger and burst through the door. "Nina!" he shouted.

"What!" Nina shouted back, startled.

"We've got to go to the hospital."

"Hello, Bob," Trey greeted him.

"Hey, Trey," Bob said, glancing at his friend. Then he turned back to Nina, "I've got to check out something at the hospital. The brain."

"The what?" Nina said, perplexed.

"The brain. We've got to check on the brain."

"*Your* brain needs checking," Nina replied, taking a drink of her shake.

Bob slid in next to her.

"Hey! Not so close," Nina said, shoving Bob away.

Bob grimaced. "In the movie, Frankenstein puts a bad brain in the monster."

"Yeah?" Nina said.

"Yeah! So we've got to find out which brain was stolen from the School of Medicine. If it's a bad brain, as I suspect it is, we're dealing with a homicidal maniac in the body of a giant."

Nina finished her shake. She wiped her lips. Then she turned to Bob. "You know, madman, sometimes I wonder if your circuitry is all crossed up. Then you come up with an idea that blows away all of my preconceived ideas about freshmen." She scooted out of the booth, nearly knocking Bob to the floor. "Let's go."

Bob looked at Trey. "Can you cover for me?"

"Yes," Trey replied. "I am supposed to work. I will do your work as well."

"Thanks." Bob followed Nina to the door. "Hey, if Joe shows up, can you let him know we had to run?"

"Sure," Trey said.

"Where are you going?" Hubert called from the counter. "You're supposed to close tonight."

Over his shoulder Bob called, "Can't. Got an urgent call from the Secret Service. Gotta guard the President tonight."

"Oh," Hubert said and turned back to the grill. Then he spun around, anger on his face. "Hey —"

But Bob was already gone.

• • •

The School of Medicine consisted of two major buildings. One was the hospital and the other was the extension school of the University of Miami. The extension school housed the classrooms, laboratories, and offices.

Since the break-in several days earlier, security had been tightened and Bob and Nina were told that they would have to receive special permission to enter the building.

"That's that," Nina said after the security guard slammed the door in their faces.

"I don't think so," Bob said. "Follow me." He jogged around the corner of the building.

Now what? Nina thought. She followed Bob to the back of the building, where she found him hoisting himself on top of a Dumpster. "What are you doing?"

Bob ignored her and peered inside the window. "It's the kitchen. No one's around."

"I'm not climbing on any Dumpster, madman."

"You just keep a lookout for the security guards." Bob shook the window, but it was locked. "Got a knife on you?"

"Yeah, right next to my pistol."

Bob hopped down, opened the Dumpster, and began rummaging around inside.

"You're not riding home in my car after that," Nina said, crossing her arms.

Bob concentrated on his search. After a few moments he said, "Eureka!" He straightened up and held out a strip of metal.

"What are you going to do with that?" Nina said.

"Saw it in an old movie."

Bob hopped back on top of the Dumpster and slid the strip of metal between the panes of glass. The windowcase had only a slip lock. Bob shoved the metal edge against the lock, which slipped out of its casing, unlocking the window.

"Care to join me?" Bob asked, reaching a hand down to Nina.

"I'll wait here and keep a lookout for the police when they arrive," Nina said.

Bob shrugged and slipped through the window. Fortunately, the school was empty of students and instructors for the day. From what Bob could tell, the security guard was back at his desk, feet propped up, either sleeping or watching television.

Bob wasn't sure where to begin looking, so he just started in the first room he came to. It was a lecture hall. The next room was another lecture hall. In fact, all the rooms he encountered were lecture halls.

"Man," Bob whispered to himself. "Where do they keep the dead bodies?"

Bob continued along till he found himself near the administration offices. He heard a loud rasping sound. He fell to his knees and slowly moved across the floor, under a large window. He peeked through the window and saw the guard sleeping, his head thrown back, mouth wide open.

Bob crawled into the room quietly. The guard had not moved. Bob's eyes darted over the contents of the desk until he spied a directory. He grabbed it and flipped through it until he found a room labeled CRANIAL DISSECTIONS.

Bob crawled out of the office, stood, and tiptoed down the hallway. When he was sure he was far enough away that the guard wouldn't hear him, he ran up to the second floor. He scanned the room numbers and stopped when he came to a sign that read CRANIAL DISSECTIONS. He pushed on the door and was surprised to find it opened easily.

The door opened into an anteroom. Through the anteroom was a door that looked like it led to a meat locker. A cold blast of air hit Bob as he opened the door and entered the most sterile room he had ever seen. Overhead fluorescent lights reflected off spotless metal, illuminating the room in an eerie silver glow.

One wall was floor-to-ceiling shelves filled with containers that held human brains in various sizes, floating in a thick but translucent amber liquid. Bob began scanning the shelves. All the containers and brains were present and accounted for.

Bob bent over and explored the ledges below. He came to an empty spot on the bottom shelf. Shards of broken glass littered a spot on the shelf labeled

"Keyoun Ruble, chess champion." The spot to the right held an empty glass container labeled "deviant." Bob smiled to himself. He had been right. Just as in the movie, Fritz had accidentally destroyed the good brain and replaced it with a deviant brain. It was almost as if he was destined to make the same mistake twice.

Bob trotted from the room and made his way to the kitchen, unconcerned about the sleeping guard. But just as he reached the door, he felt an iron grip on his shoulder, and he was spun around.

"Going somewhere?" Oscar stood facing Bob, his tight grip keeping Bob in place. "Doing a little trespassing?"

"Hey, Oscar," Bob said as calmly as he could. "Fancy meeting you here."

"We have some unfinished business." Oscar cocked back his arm. "Do you like astronomy?"

"Why?" Bob said.

"Because you're about to see some stars." Oscar's huge hand flew straight at Bob's nose.

Bob quickly jerked to the left, and Oscar's fist smacked into the steel door behind him. Oscar cried out in pain and released Bob's shoulder. The big senior backed away, clutching his bloody right hand.

Bob flung the door open and dashed to the window he'd entered through. He didn't look back to see if Oscar was following him. The only thing on his mind was escaping with his life.

4:45 P.M.
BEACH BURGER

"What exactly are you saying?" Nina said, disbelief in her voice.

"Oscar Morales is Herr Frankenstein," Bob replied without missing a beat.

"What are you talking about?" Trey said, puzzled.

Nina and Bob both ignored Trey. They were engaged in another battle of wills, and they were totally oblivious of everything else.

"Dr. James said that Oscar has a natural ability when it comes to anatomy and surgical techniques," Bob said. "Plus, Oscar has only been at Ponce High since this past September." He turned to Trey. "Am I right?"

Trey shrugged. "I believe that is correct. His grandmother said he used to be at a preparatory school in the north."

"There, you see?" Bob said.

"I see you've flipped too many burgers," Nina said. "Oscar's family has lived in San Tomas for years. His parents and my parents are friends."

"But you've never met Oscar until this year, right?" Nina sighed. "Right. So what?"

"When Oscar grabbed me at the School of Medicine, his hand was as cold as ice. That's because he's not human — he's not real."

"It doesn't make any sense," Nina said. "He's a linebacker on the football team. He's one of the most popular kids in school. How can he be Herr Frankenstein? You think he just turns into the mad scientist whenever it's convenient?"

"Why not?" Captain Bob said. He leaned back in the booth. "Have you forgotten our little encounter with the Wolf Man?"

"Just get to the point, Bob," Nina said.

"Didn't the Wolf Man take on the identity of a man who had lived in the area for years?"

Nina looked thoughtful. "Yes," she said quietly.

Bob nodded and went in for the kill. "Oscar Morales returned home from prep school at the same time that we released the monsters from their movies, and shortly after that, someone starts robbing graves of recently deceased teenagers. *Ipso facto*, Oscar Morales is Herr Frankenstein, just as Deputy Chad Barnes was the Wolf Man."

Nina leaned back. "Your Latin is terrible."

"But, I'm right, and that's what counts. Want another drink?" Bob said, standing up.

"No thanks," said Nina.

"I still do not understand," Trey said. "You are speaking about movies?"

Bob sat back down. "Yes. Old, classic horror movies. *Dracula, Frankenstein, The Wolf Man.*"

"I know it sounds impossible," Nina said. "But it's true. We accidentally released six monsters from classic movies. We've already fought Count

Dracula and the Wolf Man, and now Frankenstein has appeared. Apparently he wants you for some reason. That's why Fritz attacked you."

"I thought I had another seizure," Trey said.

"No," Bob said as he slurped the last of his drink. "You were attacked by a hunchback that looks like an ape. He said he wanted the smart one."

"Trey, do you know your IQ?" Nina asked.

"What is IQ?" Trey asked.

"Intelligence quotient. It's an exam to measure how smart you are."

"Oh, yes," Trey responded. "I was given such a test by the counselor at Ponce. One-eighty."

"One-eighty!" Bob said in disbelief.

"That's supergenius," Nina said. "That's what Fritz meant when he said the master wanted the smart one."

"Frankenstein has a rotten brain in his monster, and he must replace it with an intelligent brain," Bob added. "I found out that Fritz had stolen a defective brain from the lab. He must have dropped the good brain, because there were pieces of a broken glass container. Oscar must have returned to find a better brain since Fritz failed to get Trey's." Bob looked at Nina. "Remember Keyoun Ruble, the state chess champion a few years ago?"

"Yeah. Why?"

"It was his brain in the jar that was broken. The label was right on the shelf."

"Whose brain did Fritz take?" Nina said.

"I'm not sure," Bob said. "It was French."

"French?"

"Yeah. De something."

"De?"

"Yeah: De Viant."

"De Viant?" Nina looked puzzled. "I don't remember anyone named De Viant dying recently."

Bob snickered. Nina gave him a long look. Then her face dropped and she pursed her lips.

"De Viant!" Nina sighed. "Fifty thousand comedians out of work and you think you're Mel Brooks!"

Bob burst out laughing.

"What?" Trey asked, frowning.

"De Viant," Nina said. "Deviant. Fritz stole a deviant brain and, obviously, it was put in Captain Boob's head!"

Bob chuckled, sighed, and then his face grew serious. "The smart one," he said, looking at Trey. "Frankenstein wants that computer brain of yours."

"He cannot have it," Trey said seriously. "I am not finished with it yet."

Bob suppressed a smile and glanced at his watch. "Joe's late."

CHAPTER SIXTEEN
ONE HOUR LATER
OVER AT THE FRANKENSTEIN PLACE

"Very good, Fritz. Excellent. Now all we need is the boy, and we can bring to life a new creation, one void of diseased flesh and diseased mind." Herr Frankenstein hovered over the unconscious form of Joe Motley, who lay strapped to a gurney. "He is in excellent physical shape." The scientist's eyes gleamed. "Why didn't I think of this before? All the other bodies were dead too long. The tissue was beyond the point of regeneration. But we will preserve the flesh, and when the new brain is ready, we will have our finest creation — a superhuman whose hereditary succession will one day rule the world!"

"Yes, Master," Fritz hissed.

Herr Frankenstein looked up into the darkening sky. "Tonight will be a storm like no other. Tonight we will finally succeed where we have failed twice before. Tonight begins a new generation for a new millennium." He looked at Fritz. "Quick, bring me the other boy. With his brain and this body and my super DNA, we will perfect what was once a flawed creation."

"Yes, Master," Fritz said. He scampered from the room.

The scientist walked quickly to the desk where his new computer sat. He began typing in the commands he would need for tonight's experiment. He had learned. Twice he had failed, and twice he had learned. Now, on the third attempt, he would achieve his ultimate goal of creating life from death, of creating a human being whose potential was unlimited. He slid in a recordable CD and copied his files. He would preserve his formula for the perfect human being for history's sake, so that all the world for generations to come would know that it was he, Herr Henry Frankenstein, who had given humankind the gift of a new fire, the gift of superior strength and intelligence and immortality.

A quick noise made the scientist start. He turned as a dark shadow fell over him.

The Creature growled softly, his upper lip curled. He stared down at his creator.

Herr Frankenstein showed no fear. But he did show repulsion toward his creation. Repulsion that the brain within the monster's skull was as corrupt as the skin that was slowly decaying from the monster's body. Patches of greenish dead tissue had already fallen from the exposed arms and chest of the monstrosity, revealing blackened muscle that was shriveling with each passing hour. The Creature could not survive without Herr Frankenstein's formula, and the scientist had not seen fit to pass it on to his unworthy creation.

The scientist stood, grabbing the CD disk that held his greatest and most dreadful secrets. He moved away from the table.

The monster's eyes slowly followed the scientist as Frankenstein moved toward the gurney. With deliberation, the monster moved to the table and looked down at Joe. A sad, forlorn look came over his face. He glanced up at his creator and groaned, a deep, desolate sigh of despair. He moved his hands like a starving beggar pleading for a morsel of food.

Herr Frankenstein smirked. "You? You think you deserve such a body?" The scientist moved to the opposite side of Joe. He looked down at the teenager. "He is everything you are not." He looked at the monster. "It's not your fault. Not really. I pieced you together from the best parts of many others, thinking that the whole was greater than the sum of its parts. I've been wrong. The sum of its parts *is* the *whole*! Don't you see?"

The Creature's face went blank.

"Of course you don't, you miserable soul. Soul," the scientist continued with a laugh. "That's exactly what you lack — a soul." He looked down at Joe. "But he will have a soul. This time I have programmed not only the mechanical structure of humanity into the computer, but also the *essence* of humanity — the soul! It is the soul that separates us from the lower animals." He looked at his creation. "That separates us from all *animals*."

The monster's face seemed to age right before Herr Frankenstein. The eyes sagged and the brow drooped. Tears pooled in the corners of his eyes.

"You poor, miserable creature. I have found a new brain to go into this body. A brain that is whole and intelligent and doesn't have the mind of a criminal such as yours."

The Creature cried out, raising his hands to the darkening sky as though he were calling upon the Furies to come to his aid. He swung his arms wildly, blindly, crashing into the chains attached to the gurney.

Joe's eyes popped open. He didn't know how long he had been unconscious or exactly where he was, but he was wide-awake now. He watched as a giant of decaying flesh thrashed about the room, chasing Herr Frankenstein. At one point, the scientist stood on one side of the gurney while the monster stood on the other. Joe got a close-up view of the skin as it peeled away from the monster like a bad sunburn.

The monster tilted the gurney until it crashed over. Herr Frankenstein was thrown back and to the ground. Joe's weight broke the bindings that had held him to the gurney, and he spilled onto the floor next to the scientist. They stood simultaneously.

The monster looked at Joe, puzzled. Joe still had a sleepy look about him, but his mind had cleared enough to understand that he was in danger on two fronts: from the scientist and from the crazed creation that had accidentally freed him.

Joe shoved the scientist, and Frankenstein fell to the floor once more.

"You fool," Frankenstein screamed. "He'll kill us both."

"Now you know how I feel!" Joe yelled back. He turned to face the monster.

The Creature stood before Joe, panting, small dribbles of dark saliva oozing from the corners of his mouth. The Creature's eyes were dark and deep and uncaring. He growled and took a step toward Joe, waving a massive arm at him.

Joe had met a few people taller than him, but not many. Despite the Creature's rapidly deteriorating state, Joe knew he was no match for the living-dead giant.

Joe stepped back. He soon found himself against a cold stone wall. He edged along it, keeping his eyes on the Creature as he followed him, all the time using his peripheral vision to look for a door or any potential weapon that he could use to fight the monster.

The monster was quick. He lunged at Joe, grabbing him around the neck and lifting him from the floor.

Joe was eye to eye with death. The monster's

face had lost several strips of skin, and the muscle and tendons had blackened with decay. The monster growled and tried to smile. Joe grabbed the large wrists, taking pressure off of his throat. The monster began to shake him convulsively.

But fortunately, the Creature had forgotten about Herr Frankenstein. Joe watched over the monster's shoulder as the scientist crawled to a table a few feet away. Herr Frankenstien grabbed a syringe and drove it deep into the Creature's back. The monster howled and let go of Joe.

Joe choked and coughed. He gulped in large mouthfuls of air.

Herr Frankenstein struggled with his creation as the Creature fought against the effects of the drug. The monster was able to get on all fours. Frankenstein knelt beside him and brought his balled fists down onto the middle of the monster's back. The monster groaned, but managed to get up and stumble out the door into the black night.

Frankenstein caught his breath and slowly reached for Joe.

"You're on your own, pal," Joe said. Then he darted across the room, through the door, and out into the night.

CHAPTER SEVENTEEN

AFTER 5 P.M.
TREJO HOME

"Where have you been?" Gloria said, fear on her face, as Trey, Nina, and Bob walked through the front door of the Trejo home.

"I am okay, Gloria," Trey said, frowning. "I have been with friends. We are looking for monsters."

"What?" Gloria said, astonished. "*Tío* Miguel and *Tía* Maria are looking for you now. They are very worried. You are to stay here until they return."

"I am going with my friends."

"You will stay home!"

"Gloria," Nina said calmly, "we think that Trey is in danger."

"What danger?" Gloria said, her eyes wide with fright.

"They want my super brain," Trey said, tapping his head.

"I don't know how to explain this to you," Nina said. "There's a man who knows that Trey is very smart and he wants to take Trey's brain."

"This is unbelievable!" Gloria said. "This is impossible. This is some sort of joke."

"No," Bob said. "It's true. And Oscar Morales is the one who wants to get Trey."

"What?" asked Gloria, shocked.

Nina sighed. Then she spent the next twenty minutes explaining to Gloria about the 3-D DVD projector and how she, Joe, and Captain Bob had released the monsters from their movies. Throughout the entire explanation, Gloria looked at Nina as though she were insane.

"This cannot be," Gloria said. "Oscar is rude, but he would not harm Trey. This not a movie. This is real life. Monsters do not come out of movies. Things like this do not happen in real life."

"We're still missing something," Captain Bob said. "There's got to be more than just the storms and the access to body parts that has attracted Frankenstein and his Creature to San Tomas."

A chirping sound filled the air. Nina grabbed her cell phone and flipped it open.

"Yes," she said, and then she was quiet for several moments. "We'll be there." She headed for the door. "Let's go," she said to Bob. Then to Gloria she said, "Keep Trey here. Does your uncle have a cell phone?"

"No," Gloria said.

"Then wait for him. Keep the door locked and don't answer it. Not for anyone."

"Why?" Gloria said, trembling, but Nina was out the door.

"Where are we going?" Bob said, catching up with her. "What's wrong?"

"That was Detective Turner," Nina replied as they headed for her Camaro. "He was released earlier today. Joe's at his house."

"What's Joe doing there?"

Nina slid into the driver's seat as Bob hopped in front. "He was captured. By Herr Frankenstein."

CHAPTER EIGHTEEN
DETECTIVE TURNER'S HOME

Joe sat on the couch, telling his two friends the story he had already told Detective Turner. He finished, swallowed hard, and sat back. Exhaustion washed over him. He closed his eyes. But the images of Frankenstein and his monster danced on his closed eyelids like crazed marionettes. He opened his eyes again.

"You want anything?" Turner asked.

Joe swallowed. "Got any juice?"

Turner sat in his lounge chair. The bruises and the swelling had gone down, but were still visible. "I think."

"I'll get it," Nina said.

"Did Herr Frankenstein look like Oscar Morales?" Bob asked.

"Huh?" Joe said, looking confused.

"He thinks Oscar is Herr Frankenstein," Nina called from the kitchen.

"No," Joe said. "I didn't see Oscar around."

"Of course," Bob said to himself. "He would have transformed into Herr Frankenstein."

"I don't know about this hypothesis," Turner put in, looking doubtful.

"It's not a hypothesis when it's a fact," Bob said, trying not to sound disrespectful.

Joe thought a moment. "This sounds like what happened with the Wolf Man."

"That's what I'm saying," Bob said, happy someone finally agreed with him.

"Anything's possible," Joe said.

"Well anyway, we know what Fritz meant when he said the master wanted the smart one," Bob said.

"He wanted Trey," Joe said.

"Hey!" Bob said. "How did you know?"

"Logical guess," Joe said as he swallowed.

"Frankenstein must have figured out that he can't use dead body parts for his creature. Dead is dead, at least those who have been dead for a while."

"He's got to have flesh that has not begun to decay," Joe said. "He's got a regenerative DNA formula, but it doesn't reverse decay."

"What does it do?" asked Nina. She returned from the kitchen with a large glass of juice.

"It reinforces the DNA already in the body and gives living tissue super resilience to disease and injury," Joe explained. "He wanted to use my body because I'm young and big, but he wanted Trey's brain because Trey is a genius."

"Did you recognize the house?" Turner said.

Joe nodded. "That old mansion outside of town."

"That place hasn't been lived in nearly fifty years," Turner replied. "I'm surprised it hasn't fallen down around them."

"I say we go out there and round us up some body snatchers," Bob said eagerly.

"You remember what happened at the Carfax with Dracula?" Nina said. "If we go out there alone we'll get ourselves killed. I say we come up with a plan."

Bob begin to speak up.

"A *good* plan," Nina interrupted.

Bob frowned.

"What did Fritz say to you when he attacked you and Trey?" Turner said.

"That he wanted to eat my leg," Bob replied.

"No, about the 'smart one.'"

"Fritz said that the master wanted the smart one."

"And not the foolish one," Nina said, eyeing Bob.

Bob ignored her. Finding Frankenstein was more important than verbally sparring with Nina.

"And he grabbed Trey?" Turner said.

"Yeah," Bob said.

"What do you know about Trey?" Turner asked Bob.

"He's a refugee from Cuba," Bob said. "He's been here about four months. He's cool and he's smart."

"Four months?" Turner said. "Isn't that when

you guys stole that projector and released all those monsters?"

"Borrowed," Nina corrected. "Are you saying that Trey is mixed up in this?"

"Every time you kids have gotten involved with one of these monsters, it has turned out that one of your friends is involved as well," Turner said. "Angela Chavarria was Count Dracula's bride. From what you told me about your adventures in Wales, that rodeo queen and her boyfriend were werewolves. Now you've made friends with a Cuban refugee who just happened to show up four months ago. That's one coincidence too many."

"Trey's not a part of Frankenstein's mad scheme," Bob said defensively.

"How do you know?" Turner said. "What do you know about him?"

Bob stood. "I know he's not involved the way you say he is!"

"Calm down, Bob," Nina said. "Detective Turner's just trying to help us figure this out."

Bob breathed deeply. "Well, he's wrong about Trey."

"Do you have a copy of the original *Frankenstein*?" Joe said.

"Yes. Why?" Turner replied.

"My copy has parts missing. I want to look at a version that has all the characters. Maybe I can figure this thing out."

"It's on the shelf," Turner said, pointing at a wall

that was covered top to bottom with videotapes and DVDs. "But be careful: That's the special rereleased digitalized version with the trailer."

Joe grabbed the DVD. "Can you give me a ride home?" he asked Nina.

"Careful," Turner warned as he walked them all to the door. "Looks like another storm is about to hit." He watched as they walked to Nina's car. "Call me if you figure anything out."

Nina was about to put the car in drive when Turner hobbled up to Joe's window. He tapped on the glass, and Joe rolled the window down.

"I've got one question I want you three to think about," Turner said. "Just by looking at Joe, it's obvious why Herr Frankenstein would want him as a part of his experiment. He's big, strong, agile, physically fit, and coordinated."

"So, what's the question?" Bob said impatiently.

"How did Herr Frankenstein know that Trey had a genius brain to put inside that large body? You can't tell if someone's a genius just by looking at him."

Joe, Bob, and Nina were silent.

"It's obvious," Turner continued, "that Frankenstein is going to try to create another creature, this time using Joe and Trey. He needs another body and another brain. This time, he needs them as close to perfection as possible."

"I don't know if I should feel flattered or scared to death," Joe said.

"Be scared," Bob said. "Be very scared."

Turner waved as the trio drove off.

They drove in silence for several minutes, and then Bob finally blurted out, "Turner's wrong about Trey. What possible evidence does he have to suspect him?"

"Maybe it's just a policeman's gut instinct," Nina replied.

"Maybe when you two were playing Young Frankenstein with that frog in lab," Joe said. "Trey knew what he was doing without looking at the book or being told."

"That still doesn't explain how Frankenstein found out about Trey's genius," Nina said.

They rode in silence, and a few minutes later Bob was standing in the driveway of his uncle's beach house, waving to his friends.

He went into the house. He was glad his mother wasn't home. She would not be happy that he had left Hubert alone at the Beach Burger.

He went back into the large TV room, where he had made himself a pallet on the floor, and threw himself on top of the quilts. He listened to the rumble of the thunder from outside and was soon lulled to sleep.

CHAPTER NINETEEN
LATER THAT NIGHT
THE MONSTER'S SHED

The Creature sat petting his dead dog. The dog's black eyes stared into nothingness, a yellow ooze the consistency of custard dripping from the corner of his eyes. The monster had failed to kill the man who had created him and now wanted to kill him. His befuddled mind was a mixture of images past and present, blurred by the fog that never left his brain. Voices echoed through his skull but the monster could not make out distinct words, only metallic groans and shrill screams.

The sky roared with thunder and lit up with a brilliant arc of fire. The monster softly growled and lifted a decaying palm to the sky. He got to his knees and peered up through the cracks in the slants. Nothing. Only darkness.

He crawled out of the shed just as rain began to fall. He lifted his face and let the wetness wash over him, soothing his seething brow. He had learned that the water from the sky was his friend. He had learned also that the roar from the sky was not challenging him but welcoming him. He had learned that the fire that struck through the darkness had given him life. The fire was his mother. And tonight she spoke to him. She shouted from the heavens and wrote upon the clouds what he was to do.

The Creature smiled. He turned and walked away from the shed and his dead dog.

This time, he wouldn't be going back to his creator. The man wanted to destroy him and replace him, but he wouldn't let that happen.

With a fierce determination, the monster set off in search of the two boys whom the creator now favored. The monster smiled. The two boys would be no good to the creator if they were torn limb from limb.

JOE'S HOUSE
MIDNIGHT

Joe hit the OFF button and then REWIND on the remote control. The videotape stopped, reset itself with a metallic click, and then hummed as the machine rewound the tape. He had watched the movie twice before he found what he was looking for. Now that he was sure, he didn't feel any better. He thought perhaps once he had confirmed his suspicions, he'd be at ease and maybe be able to sleep. But he wasn't, and he couldn't.

Joe yawned and stretched. His eyes ached. He got up and threw himself on his bed. He didn't look forward to telling Bob what he had found out. Bob was ferociously loyal to his friends, sometimes to a fault. Joe tried to think of different ways to tell his best friend the bad news. When he couldn't, Joe turned over to his side and was soon asleep.

CHAPTER TWENTY
FRIDAY, 1:30 P.M.
MS. BASHARA'S ENGLISH CLASS

"Speak to me what thou art."

"Thy evil spirit, Brutus," Captain Bob replied. He wore a bloodstained toga wrapped around him, and his face and hands were covered in white clown makeup. Although he only had three lines and would be onstage for no more than ten seconds, Act IV scene iii of *Julius Caesar* was Bob's favorite because he got to be Caesar's Ghost. Bob had wanted to add bloody gashes and decaying skin to his face and arms, but Ms. Bashara wouldn't allow it.

To Bob's chagrin, Megan McMahan was in charge of makeup for the dress rehearsal. Bob had winced in pain several times as she applied the white cake makeup with a rough sponge. He also accused her of purposely poking him in the eye as she applied the eyeliner. Megan swore her innocence, but Bob knew it was her attempt at revenge for burning up her weave.

Bob had a plan, though. On the night of the

freshman class play, he would let Megan make him up as Caesar's Ghost just as Ms. Bashara wanted, but before going onstage, he would secretly add the bloody gashes, dripping blood, and yellow pus that any respectable dead ghost would have.

They finished the fourth act, and Bob was dismissed to the rest room to wash off his makeup.

"Help me out," Bob said to Joe as he left the room. After they entered the rest room, Bob said, "So, you want to tell me what's up?"

Joe sighed.

"You didn't say two words at breakfast or lunch," Bob said as he scrubbed the makeup from his face. "Did you find anything in the film to help us?"

"I'm still checking things out."

Bob frowned. "What? You're not going to tell me what you're thinking? I suppose you've told Nina."

"I haven't told anybody. I don't want to tell anybody until I know for certain."

"Two heads are better than one," Bob said, drying off his face.

"Let me check out something first, and I'll tell you in biology."

The bell rang. Joe sighed again, this time from relief. "I've got to get to gym class. Do you have to go to work after school?"

"Yes. So does Trey. I'm going to stick close to him until we find Herr Frankenstein and Fritz and put an end to this."

"Later, madman."

"Yeah," Bob said with a scowl. Bob didn't know what his friend knew, but he didn't like the fact that Joe didn't trust him enough to confide in him. He had seen Joe and Nina talking in the hallway between classes and when he had approached them, they had acted guilty, as though he had caught them talking about him.

Bob frowned, grabbed his backpack, and burst out through the rest room door and into the noisy, crowded hallway of Ponce High.

Joe tucked in his gym shirt and headed out the door to the basketball court. He hadn't lied to his best friend, but it felt as though he had. He was grateful to have P.E. now. His energy level was high, as was his level of frustration, and gym was just what he needed to work off both. He was glad Bob would be occupied after school. That would give him time to confirm his suspicions.

Joe trotted out onto the basketball court. A couple of other boys were shooting baskets at the other end of the court. P.E., like band, art, choir, drama, and other so-called electives, was slowly and surely being phased out of the Ponce High curriculum and replaced by courses like computer programming and social economics. So only a few students were enrolled in P.E., just enough to keep the class going for one more year. Joe knew that next year there probably wouldn't even be a P.E. class. He didn't know what he would do then. He enjoyed pickup games of basketball or sandlot football, but he didn't like playing organized sports. The emphasis on winning was too high.

A smaller boy threw the ball to Joe.

"Dunk it, big man!" the boy yelled.

Joe dribbled and walked to the basket, slowly at first. The closer he got, the faster and harder he dribbled and the quicker his pace became. When he was six feet from the hoop, Joe leaped, cradling the ball in one hand, and did his best to imitate Air Jordan, tongue and all. He twisted his hand and the ball turned over. He flicked his wrist and the ball sailed through the hoop, barely touching the net as it rocketed through the hole.

He hit the floor and pulled up his gym shorts.

"Awright, big man," the shorter student said.

Since the coach was usually busy with varsity players, Joe and the others got to play basketball or anything else they wanted. The others usually followed Joe's lead, and today, he felt like playing basketball.

The period passed quickly, and Joe was soon dressed and sitting on a bench leaning against a row of lockers, waiting for the bell.

Why wait until after school? Joe thought. He glanced at his watch. He had ten minutes before the bell rang. He could go to the school library, get on the Internet, and confirm what he had suspected since late the previous night.

Joe stood up to go, and then he heard a locker

bang. He'd thought he was alone in the locker room.

"Hey," Joe called out.

No answer.

He heard a shuffling several rows over.

"Hey," Joe called out. "What's up?"

Heavy breathing accompanied the shuffling.

Joe sighed. He was tired of these games. Several times already, some of the varsity players had sneaked up on him and tried to take him down. Joe had no problem with his size, but it seemed that others did and for some reason they wanted to prove the adage "The bigger they are, the harder they fall." Only Joe didn't fall too easily. He had been taunted and teased about his height since the sixth grade, and usually all he had to do was scowl and the taunting and teasing would stop. That worked in junior high, but high school was a different story. In high school, the upperclassmen didn't give up and they didn't learn their lesson very well. Joe had tangled with a group of them the first week of school and came out on top, and still they kept after him, each time with Joe emerging the least bruised.

Joe stood. Maybe this would be the last time. Maybe he ought to really let himself get mad and unleash on his tormentors. Maybe that would end it all.

Nah, he thought with a shake of his head.

"Awright, boys," Joe said. "You can stop your sneaking around because I'm leaving for class."

The heavy breathing and shuffling ceased.

Joe grabbed his backpack and started toward the door.

A metal creaking resonated in the locker room. Puzzled, Joe stopped. He saw the row of lockers falling toward him just in time to drop his gym bag and put both hands against the lockers. With a grunt, he stopped them from falling. With another grunt, he pushed the lockers and they righted themselves. But then a metallic bang exploded in the air, and the lockers flew back at Joe. He fell to the ground as the lockers continued to fall and strike the lockers behind him, forming a metal tent above him.

This prank was getting dangerous. Joe decided to crawl out from under the lockers and run out the door. He grabbed his backpack and began crawling. He looked up as he crawled out of the opening and found himself staring into the decaying face of Frankenstein's monster.

The monster growled, reached down, and pulled Joe to his feet. He was a full head taller than Joe.

Without hesitation, Joe struck the monster with a right cross. His hand hit soft, mushy flesh and then connected with hard bone. The bone cracked with the force of the blow and the monster's head twisted to the side.

The monster slowly turned his head and stared at Joe. His mouth opened into an evil grin. A black ooze dripped from the cracked lips and gums. Bits of broken teeth from Joe's blow fell from his mouth. Then the smile dropped from the monster's face and he began to shake Joe like a rag doll.

The scene around Joe became one crazy mixture of color as the monster shook him. He felt as though his brain was bouncing off the sides of his skull. Joe swung out again, this time with both fists. His hands struck both sides of the monster's dead face simultaneously. The monster yelled and let go of him.

Joe tried to scramble to his feet, but his head still swam with dizziness. He looked up and thought he saw two monsters standing over him. The black ooze seemed to flow out of two gashes on either side of the monster's face.

The Creature reached down and grabbed Joe by the throat. He pulled the teen up by the neck and held him above the ground. Joe struggled with the monster's grip, but to no avail.

The monster gurgled a laugh.

Before the darkness and the nightmares completely overtook him, Joe thought he saw Trey standing behind the monster.

CHAPTER TWENTY-ONE

Trey grabbed Joe's fallen backpack and swung at the middle of the monster's back. The monster was knocked into the lockers. Then Trey slammed the heavy book bag into the monster's head. The Creature slumped to the ground and remained motionless.

Trey kneeled down and put his arm under Joe. "Wake up, Joe. We must leave quickly."

Joe groaned.

"Let us go, *mi amigo*." Trey pulled at his friend.

Joe slowly stood and then fell back against the lockers. Trey draped the large freshman's arm around his neck and began walking him out of the locker room. Joe tried to help, but found it hard to coordinate his legs. He felt a rising sickness in the pit of his stomach.

Trey half-walked, half-dragged his friend out of the locker room and down the empty hallway. Trey wanted to get as far away from the monster as possible.

Where was a teacher when you needed one? Trey thought. Joe was heavy and Trey didn't know how much longer he could help him.

A growl echoed down the hallway. Trey turned slightly and saw the monster emerge from the gym. He tried to speed up.

"I need you to help me, Joe," Trey said, panting. He saw the monster coming nearer out of the corner of his eye. "Wake up, Joe. He is getting closer."

Joe groaned. The sickness moved from the pit of his stomach and up into his throat. He gagged, but nothing came up. The stinging acid in his throat brought Joe back to his senses. He began to move himself forward at a slow trot.

Trey felt the weight lift from his shoulders and he, too, began to pick up speed. He turned slightly. The monster was gaining on them.

"Hey!" Trey yelled down the hallway. "Hey!" The shout echoed off the lockers and the walls.

A door opened. "What's going on out —" Ms. Bashara began. Then she screamed when she saw the monster just behind the two boys.

Trey and Joe dashed into the English classroom. Ms. Bashara slammed the door.

"What's happening?" the teacher demanded.

"Call the police," Trey yelled. "It is a monster."

Ms. Bashara screamed and jumped away from the door as the wood splintered behind her. She ran behind her desk. Joe and Trey ran to the windows and tried to unlock them.

A loud thump came from the door. It bowed and then split in two.

The windows refused to open. Joe grabbed a chair and began pounding the window with the legs. The thick, steel-reinforced glass failed to break. Trey grabbed a chair and joined in.

The monster staggered to the two boys. His eyes were bright and a fiendish smile crossed his face.

The boys turned and threw their chairs at the monster as he approached. The monster easily batted them away.

The monster lurched forward and grabbed Trey. The Creature wrapped his arms around him and lifted him from the floor. Trey groaned as the monster's crunching embrace squeezed against his rib cage.

Joe swung out and hit the monster in the nose. The nose flattened with a sickening sound as the cartilage broke in two. The monster was unfazed.

Trey's face began to slowly change from a healthy tan to a yellowish brown.

Joe hit the monster again, and again the monster was unfazed. But he let loose with one hand and hit Joe on the side of the head.

Stars exploded in Joe's head and he fell to the ground. The last thing he saw was the monster crashing through the window, Trey still held in his arms.

CHAPTER TWENTY-TWO
DR. JAMES'S CLASSROOM

"That's very good, Captain Bob," Dr. James said as he stood over Bob and the dissected frog.

Sweat beaded on Bob's forehead and dripped into his eyes. Bob shook his head and blinked. The salt in the sweat stung his eyes. He had spent the last thirty minutes suturing the frog's arm back onto its shoulder. Dr. James had spent the entire class working with him while other students either explored their dissected frogs or sat looking bored.

"Thanks, Dr. James," Bob said, sitting back, proud of his work. "I thought Oscar would be here today," Bob continued, hoping his voice was calm. He hadn't seen Oscar all day, which made him all the more suspicious that Oscar was the madman they were looking for. He was probably just laying low.

"I don't know where he is," Dr. James replied. "I'm disappointed in him. Like you, he's got a good mind, but he tends to be lazy when it comes to mental exertion."

"Mmm," Bob said. "You notice anything funny about him?"

"Nothing out of the ordinary," Dr. James said. "Now Bob, I was wondering if you would like to help with something after school today."

"I don't know. I'm supposed to go to work."

"Well, I'm tutoring some students from the School of Medicine and I think you'd enjoy what we're doing."

"What is it?"

Dr. James smiled. "You interested in working on a human body?"

Bob sat up. "You mean a real live dead human body?"

"Yes. Some students have finals coming up on anatomy and we're going over some of the more intricate surgical procedures. You can't actually do anything because of state law, but you can observe."

The bell rang. Students poured from the classroom without waiting for permission to leave.

"My bike's broken."

"That's all right. You can ride with me."

"Cool," Bob said, putting his yacht cap on his head. He could always be a little late for work — Trey would cover for him. "Ready when you are, Doc."

Dr. James laughed and headed for the door.

"What about your lab coat?" Bob said, joining him. "You're still wearing it."

The doctor looked down, perplexed. "Oh, I forgot. I guess I'm the typical absentminded professor." He chuckled. "I'll need it anyway."

Minutes later, they were in Dr. James's car and headed out of the parking lot.

"Man, this is an ancient car," Bob said, looking over the interior. "What's all that dirt back there?"

"Sometimes I have to dig up the cadavers the students use myself," Dr. James replied, grinning.

"Yeah, right," Bob said with a smirk. He turned back around. "Hey, what kind of radio is this?" He leaned forward and twisted a cracked plastic knob. The radio hummed and hissed to life. Ranchero music blared through the speakers. "You listen to this stuff? I have to listen to ranchero music for my Spanish class. I don't understand the language when it's spoken, let alone when it's sung."

Dr. James laughed. "I never play the radio. I guess the last owner must have had it on that station."

"Hey," Bob said, looking around. "Aren't we going to the School of Medicine?"

"No," Dr. James said. "The students are meeting me at my house. I've got the cadaver there."

"That's creepy having a dead body at your house," Bob said with a grimace.

"Not as noisy as a wife or as troublesome as a pet." Dr. James laughed again. Bob decided to tell Nina about Dr. James's slight against wifehood. It was sure to get a rise out of her.

"Here we are," Dr. James said as they pulled into a long, narrow driveway.

"I've seen this from the road, but I've never been here," Captain Bob said as they neared the mansion. "I thought it was deserted."

"It was," Dr. James said as he pulled up in front of the Goldstadt Mansion. He climbed out of the car.

Bob climbed out, too, and stared up at the mansion. Something felt off. *The old mansion outside of town.* It was like a mental itch he couldn't scratch. He turned to ask Dr. James about it, when suddenly he felt a sharp pain at the back of his head. And then everything went dark.

CHAPTER TWENTY-THREE
AT THE FRANKENSTEIN PLACE

Bob felt something tightening around his wrists. He moaned and slowly opened his eyes.

He tried to get up but found himself held down by ropes across his chest and legs. Fritz smiled at him, the yellow, rotten teeth inches from his face.

Bob looked around quickly. A computer rested on a desk against one wall. A hospital gurney was attached to chains that led up to a high ceiling that opened on the dark sky. Bob spotted Dr. James and tried to speak. A fire burned in his throat and all he could manage was a gurgle.

Dr. James turned around. "Oh, you're awake," he said as he walked up to the table to which Bob was strapped down.

Bob watched with wide-eyed amazement as Dr. James took off his lab coat. Bob had never seen his favorite teacher without the lab coat. Now he could see that the coat was lined with stuffing that gave the teacher a pudgy look. Dr. James was not short: He was actually stooped over.

Now his teacher straightened to his full height. Then he began to tug at his forehead. Bob gasped as the doctor's skin peeled away.

"Herr Frankenstein!" Bob gasped.

"Yes, my friend," Frankenstein said with a wry smile.

Bob looked around as best as he could. Of course, the Goldstadt Mansion. The final connection they'd been looking for. Herr Frankenstein had been drawn to the mansion because of its name — it was the same name as the town he'd grown up in.

Bob gasped when he realized there was a body lying on a gurney several feet away. It was Oscar Morales. He was unconscious, breathing shallowly.

"What is Oscar doing here?" Bob asked.

"Your friend Joe was my first choice, but he escaped. Oscar is in top physical shape. He will do." The scientist flung back the sheet covering Oscar to reveal wires attached to his skin. "It's a shame, really. I'll have to destroy his brain. And he's really rather intelligent. But I need his body more."

"I thought I was going to help you," Bob said slowly, swallowing to put out the fire in this throat.

"You *are* going to help me, my friend," Frankenstein replied.

Fritz gurgled a laugh. "The foolish one will do, yes, Master?"

"Yes, Fritz," Frankenstein said, patting the hunchback's head. "The foolish one will do."

"What?" Bob said.

"I need a new brain," the scientist said without hesitation. "I wanted Trey's. I had checked the school records and found out that he was a genius. You were my first choice until Trey came along. After him, you've got the highest IQ at the high school."

"Thanks," Bob said with a grimace. The fire in his throat subsided. He deduced that he had been knocked unconscious, probably with some sort of knockout drug, which accounted for the small pinprick pain at the base of his skull. He couldn't remember anything after pulling up in front of the Goldstadt Mansion.

Fritz picked up a scalpel. "Let me cut open his skull. Please, Master."

"No, Fritz," the scientist said, as a father would to a child. "We will not make the same mistake twice." The scientist grabbed hair clippers and flipped them on, the buzz echoing slightly through the large room. He put the clippers to Bob's head and began cutting off the teenager's mop top.

"Hey!" Bob protested, but he couldn't move.

"Amazing world, this twenty-first century," Frankenstein said. Clumps of hair fell to the floor. "We did dream of such advances in technology in my world. Not only have scientists today given us the basic code to life itself — DNA — but amazing computers and the capability to transfer knowledge from one computer to another." He continued to shave Bob's head. "And what is the brain, really?

Just another computer. The greatest computer on Earth. I will transfer your brain's knowledge to another body."

"Yeah?" Bob said as the clippers furrowed his unkempt hair. "Who'd you have in mind? I don't see any extra bodies lying around."

"You teenagers are as inconsistent as you are foolish," the mad scientist replied. "Your friends will come looking for you."

"Joe," Bob whispered, terrified.

"Yes," Frankenstein replied. "And then I will prove once and for all that I am as great as any god who dared to tread the heavens. I will bring a new fire to humankind!" The mad scientist laughed long and hard.

Bob watched the clippers slide past his eyes several times. He felt a cold draft on his newly shorn head.

"Huh?" Frankenstein said with a start. He stopped his cutting and spun around. Bob followed his gaze.

The monster had burst through the door carrying Trey in his decaying arms.

Fritz growled and lurched toward the monster, who dropped the unconscious boy. Bob watched as the two wrestled. Although half the size of the monster, Fritz was just as strong, and his lower center of gravity gave him an advantage over the taller and much heavier monster.

The monster had Fritz by the throat, but he didn't appear to be defeating the hunchback. Fritz reached out and tugged at the monster's hair. A tuft of hair and skin pulled away from the monster's head, revealing a yellowed, cracked skull. The monster yelled and dropped Fritz.

Herr Frankenstien picked up a syringe from the computer table and jabbed it into the monster's neck. The monster screamed again and turned, swinging his arms wildly. The scientist ducked. Fritz laughed maniacally and stuck his leg out, tripping the tall creature. The monster fell to the floor with a thud and lay still.

Moments later, Frankenstein and Fritz had the monster tied to the gurney. Frankenstein finished tying the rope and walked over to his computer. He put a CD into the machine's drive and waited.

The drive hummed and whirred. Frankenstein watched as the screen jumped to life. Coded DNA ran across his screen in letters of G, A, T, and C — strand after strand of computer-enhanced enzyme molecules that made up the basis of all life.

"If you could only see the glory that is written upon this screen," he said to Bob, his voice high-pitched and cracking. "The difference between a human and an ape is less than two percent of DNA, but what a difference that small difference makes. It gives humans the ability to talk, to move an opposable thumb, to reason, to imagine, to dream, to create.

"Before, in the other time and the other place," he continued, "I had thought a special ray held the secret of life. But here, in this brave new world, I have learned that simple DNA is the key. Simple in structure, complex in formation. Just like a human being.

"DNA is the key, but it only unlocks the door. To push the door open, I needed something else, something that I had failed to recognize the first two times I created a living being from dead tissue."

Bob struggled against the ropes but still could not get loose.

"In every culture on every continent on Earth, the creation stories resound with a simple and profound truth," Frankenstein continued. "In each case, the creator-being breathed life into its creation, either directly or through a great wind. And in each case this word *breathe* was also translated as the word *spirit*. This, then, is what I had missed when I attempted to join the great creator-beings. I had neglected to breathe life into my creation, to give it a soul.

"This time I will not only give my creation life, I will give my creation a soul." The mad scientist stopped his typing, stood, and walked over to Bob. "Your soul. I have my brain. That beast unwittingly delivered him to me." He nodded toward Trey. "His brain and your soul, Captain Bob."

Herr Frankenstein stared down at the monster on the gurney. "With his brain and your heart," he declared, "I will give a new birth to the future of humankind!"

"But in class you said I didn't have the heart," Bob retorted.

"You don't have the heart to push yourself in your studies," Frankenstein said. "But with your friends, you are loyal to the core. It is a rare thing today to find a person who will sacrifice himself for his friends. That is the part of you I will place in my Creature."

Frankenstein turned and lifted a scalpel from the table behind him. The sharp edge glinted in the overhead light. Herr Frankenstein looked up into the loft that opened out into the sky. Night was settling upon the earth. Tonight's storm would not be strong enough for his purposes. He would have to wait until tomorrow.

He turned back to the bodies lying before him.

Never mind. He had work enough tonight.

He put the scalpel to the monster's head and gently pressed down.

The monster's eyes shot open, and he groaned.

Startled, Frankenstein stepped back, reaching his left hand behind him to grab the syringe on the table.

With one swift movement, the monster broke his bindings, swung his legs around, and was on his feet.

Frankenstein held the syringe like a knife and brought it down. But the monster caught his hand before the needle could meet its target. The monster squeezed and twisted the scientist's wrist.

Frankenstein grimaced and cried out in pain. The monster slowly but surely forced him to the floor.

The monster stood over him triumphantly. Frankenstein held his wrist. He could feel the broken bones. He looked up into the monster's face. Patches of skin were peeling off. The eyelids were all but gone, giving the monster a blank, distant look.

Frankenstein sneered. "All right. If you're going to kill me, kill me quickly and be done with it. I'm sick of looking at you!"

The monster's eyes softened, and Frankenstein saw a look of bewilderment and pain in his face. The monster held his hands toward the scientist, palms up, like a starving beggar asking for a morsel of food.

Frankenstein sat back, perplexed, still holding his broken wrist.

Then a look of acceptance crossed the monster's face. His eyes watered and he sighed. The beast stood to his full height, turned, and walked out of the room into the black of night.

Frankenstein still sat on the floor holding his wrist. His mind was a knot of confusion. The beast he had created, the monster he had set loose upon the world, had tried to communicate with him, but what did he want? What in the name of heaven did the monster want?

CHAPTER TWENTY-FOUR

Nina nosed the car to the edge of the driveway that led up to the Goldstadt Mansion. A chill ran down her spine. This was déjà vu all over again, just like their battle with Count Dracula at the Carfax Hotel. She was grateful that this time the monster could not change into a wolf, a giant bat, a mist, or anything else. Frankenstein and his creature were susceptible to all the hazards of a normal person. No need for crosses, stakes, silver bullets, holy water, pentagrams, or wolfsbane. Just good old-fashioned brains and brawn.

And having Detective Turner with his .357 was an added advantage as well. Turner may not be as big and strong as Joe, but the gun spoke volumes.

"Let's hope we get there before Trey loses his mind," Joe said.

"That's not funny, Joe. You're beginning to sound like Captain Bob," Nina said, hopping out of the car.

"It wasn't meant to be funny," Joe said innocently, getting out after his friend.

"You two cool it," Turner said. "We've got more important things to do. This place is supposed to be deserted," Turner continued as they slowly approached the building. "The Goldstadts died without leaving an heir."

The Goldstadt Mansion had been built in the 1920s. Back then, it was the place to be seen by the social elite. It was truly a castle, brought over stone by stone by the eccentric multimillionaire. It even had a moat and a drawbridge. The front of the castle faced south, while each wing had two towers that pushed against the sky. Goldstadt had died, and then his wife died, and then the mansion began to slowly decay with time.

"Somebody's made himself at home," Joe said, pointing to the light coming from the western tower. He held the camera in his left hand, but he wasn't sure if it would work.

The first two monsters they'd fought were different from the Frankenstein monster. Dracula and the Wolf Man dwelled in the ether world of the spiritual. The Frankenstein monster was pure flesh and blood, stitched together and given life by a madman who wanted to prove to the world that he was a god.

Strangely, Joe understood the motivation behind the vampire and the werewolf, but what motivated the monster? Herr Frankenstein was motivated by vanity. What about the monster? What did he want? Joe's mind flashed through the movie he had viewed twice the night before. Something had struck him the second time through — something he should have figured out much earlier. It was Herr Frankenstein's obsession with life. Only one person Joe could think of shared that obsession — Dr. James.

Joe couldn't believe he hadn't thought of it earlier. It was so obvious. It all fit together: the teacher had just started at Ponce High that fall. He was a medical doctor, fully trained in human anatomy. And he had full access to all the students' files — that was how he knew about Trey's IQ.

Trey. He was too late to save Trey. And now Dr. James and Bob were missing. Joe didn't like the idea that they were both gone at the same time.

Joe had regained consciousness in Ms. Bashara's class to find Detective Turner and Nina kneeling beside him. He had hurriedly explained what had happened and his suspicions about Dr. James. A quick check of the computer records of the University of Miami teaching staff and a peek in Dr. James's teaching file confirmed his suspicions. Turner used his authority to get the school secretary to let them look at the file.

Now Joe, Nina, and Turner worked their way to the back of the mansion. Joe found a door leading into the cellar and, with little effort, he pried the lock from the rotten wood. Turner flicked on his flashlight, the beam illuminating dusty concrete stairs. They walked silently and breathed as quietly as possible. The cellar was a fog of dust, draped in ancient gray cobwebs that hung from the rafters. Across the dank room, they found a set of stairs leading up from the cellar. A large double door made of dark wood stood at the top.

They quietly ascended the stairs. Joe slowly turned the cold knob. He opened the door ever so slightly. A thin ray of light appeared in the crack of the door and muffled voices could be heard. Joe could see Fritz and the scientist hovering over a table. Herr Frankenstein was mumbling orders to his assistant, who worked as quickly as his deformed body would let him, handing the scientist surgical instruments.

Joe slowly closed the door. "They're in there," he said in a barely audible whisper. "They're operating on someone."

"Trey?" Nina said.

"I couldn't see. They were in front of the table."

"Can we sneak up on them?" Nina asked.

"We need a diversion," Turner said.

"You should do it," Nina said. "Joe's the only one strong enough to get Trey off the table. You're not recovered enough."

Turner took a deep, silent breath. "All right. I'll go around to the front and sneak in that way. I'll draw them away from the table." Turner started down the stairs, his gun at the ready.

Joe and Nina looked at each other. "I'm scared," Joe whispered.

"Me too," Nina replied. "But we can do this. We've done it before."

"We always had Bob before," Joe said. "It feels wrong to do this without him."

Nina nodded, a grim look of determination on her face. "That's why we've got to get him back."

Turner didn't have any trouble entering the front of the old castle. The drawbridge was down and the door was open, barely hanging on its hinges. The night wind had pushed the few dark clouds aside and let in enough moonlight to see by.

He tiptoed down the hallway leading to the west tower. He wasn't sure what he was going to do to divert Herr Frankenstein and his hunchbacked henchman. First he wanted to get a good look at what the two fiends were doing. Hopefully, Trey wasn't on that gurney.

A sliver of light from the doorway guided him the final few steps to the west tower. He took a deep breath, held it, and then peered in through the crack.

What he saw there made Turner gasp. Lying on three tables were Captain Bob, Trey, and Oscar, their heads completely shaved. Wires from Oscar's body and Trey's head were attached to a SCSI connection at the back of a computer, which hummed and buzzed with power. Bob, Trey, and Oscar looked lifeless, their skin ashen.

Turner took a deep breath, then burst into the room. "Police!" he yelled. "Hands up and down on the floor." He held his .357 as steady as he could.

Fritz growled and stepped toward Turner. But before he could get very far, Joe and Nina lunged into the room, brandishing makeshift weapons. Fritz spun around, confused.

"Not this time, buzzard breath," Turner said, cocking the hammer on the .357.

"Do as he says, Fritz," Frankenstein said. A moment later, they both were lying on the ground, their arms spread out to their sides.

Nina and Joe stepped past them. They unhooked the wires from Bob and Trey and loosened their bonds. Bob stirred and, with Joe's help, he sat up.

"What's happening?" Bob said, rubbing his eyes.

"We're here to rescue you, madman," Joe said.

"Good," Bob said, his voice sleepy. "I was hoping we'd go to the beach today."

Joe smiled down at his friend.

"Trey," Nina said, gently holding his shoulders.

"Hello, Nina," Trey said dryly. "What is happening?"

Captain Bob stood and staggered to the table holding Trey. "They were going to use your brain to make another monster."

Turner reached for his portable police radio and

flipped it on. "Station, this is Turner," He held the small radio away from him, waiting for the reply. He pressed the button again. "Station, this is Turner. I have a priority situation. Need backup." He released the button, but again the radio remained silent. "Blazes!" Turner shouted, shaking the radio. "I think my battery's dead." He turned to Nina. "Call for backup."

Nina pulled out her cell phone. She hit the ON button and then began to dial. She put the phone to her ear. "There's no tone. The battery's good. I just changed it this morning."

"It's the walls and all this electronic equipment," Joe said. "It's causing interference. You'll have to go outside."

Nina walked out of the west tower and into the hallway. She turned her phone on and began punching numbers when a hand like a steel vise grabbed her wrist. She screamed as she dropped the phone. Then she was lifted from the ground.

The monster carried Nina by her arm back into the makeshift laboratory. He dropped her next to Bob. Her friend caught her before she could fall to the ground.

Bob looked at the Creature. His skin had turned a bluish-black, like a sick bruise, and large chunks of skin on his arms and neck and face had decayed, revealing black and torn muscle. The skin around his eyes had completely fallen off and Bob could see the eye muscles constricting and contracting as the monster looked around the room.

The monster stepped past Bob and Nina and looked down at Trey. He curled his upper lip, a mordant smile creasing his gray-green face. He stepped toward the scientist.

Frankenstein looked up from the floor, his head twisted around.

"Stop right there," Turner ordered.

The Creature kept moving toward the prostrate doctor.

"Stop, or I'll shoot!"

The monster either didn't hear or didn't care.

Turner's .357 exploded. A gaping hole appeared in the monster's left shoulder. But the monster kept moving. Turner was ready to fire again when the monster swung out and hit him in the head. Turner fell to the floor and did not move.

Frankenstein yelled and jumped up, running across the room to the doors. But the monster was just as fast. He quickly had the scientist in his grasp. He turned Frankenstein and gripped him by the throat. The scientist gagged and struggled.

Suddenly, Fritz was up, beating the monster's back and screaming. But the monster was undeviating in his purpose. Fritz picked up a chair and was about to strike the monster when the chair was yanked from his hands. Fritz spun around.

Joe held the chair with one hand while his other

was balled into a fist. "I owe you this," and with that he unleashed a right jab, flattening Fritz's nose with a sickening crunch. Fritz cried out and clutched at his face as blood spurted from his nostrils. Joe grabbed the neck brace and spun the hunchback around. Fritz yelled as he flew across the room. He grabbed the metal wheel, trying to right himself. The wheel spun and the platform upon which Frankenstein and his monster were fighting rose into the air.

"The camera, Bob!" Nina yelled.

Bob aimed the camera at the ascending combatants. He flipped open the viewfinder, pushed the RECORD button, and watched as creator and creation battled for life and death.

But nothing happened. The two continued to battle.

"It's not working," Bob yelled. "They're not being sucked in!"

"Zoom in!" Nina called.

"I am! Nothing's happening!"

Lightning snaked across the sky, silhouetting Frankenstein and the Creature. The Creature still had Frankenstein by the throat.

"No!" Fritz yelled. He ran toward the chains. Joe tried to grab him, but Fritz was able to leap over Joe and grab one of the chains. Like a chimpanzee, Fritz ascended the fifty feet to help his master fight off the monster.

"What are we going to do?" Bob yelled at Joe.

"The camera's not working! They're not changing back."

Lightning ignited the loft, sending sparks flying as it hit the rigging and the chains.

"Look!" Nina said, pointing at the platform.

The monster was transformed into the Frankenstein monster: thick hobnailed boots, flat head, ugly scar running from the top of his head to the large overhanging brow, green skin, and two smoking electrodes protruding from his neck.

The Frankenstein monster fought his creator and Fritz. He held Herr Frankenstein with one hand and with the other shoved Fritz off the platform. Fritz stumbled backward and grabbed empty air in an attempt to balance himself. He flew off the platform and into the chains. A chain wrapped about his neck as he fell, and he jerked to a stop. His neck was broken, just like in the movie.

Lightning flashed again and this time the thunder was right behind it.

"The computer!" Joe yelled as he saw the monitor flicker to life. He ran to the machine, closely followed by Nina and Bob. He sat at the keyboard and watched the screen. Strings of G's, A's, T's, and C's ran across the screen and wrapped down to the next line. Soon they were moving so quickly that they were practically a blur. Joe grabbed a CD, opened the CD drawer, and shoved the recordable disk into the computer.

Lightning burned in the dark sky. Thunder

clapped and shook the platform. The whole plat-form was alight in an angelic haze as monster and madman fought each other.

Joe hit the ESCAPE key and the computer screen went blank. He moved the cursor to the video icon and double-clicked. The monitor spurted, and a video editing screen wavered into focus.

Lightning hit the platform again. And this time the two opponents began to glow with the same white haze as the platform.

"We've got to reverse the process!" Joe shouted above the roar of thunder. "We've got to record them on the disk." He moved the cursor to the RECORD button and clicked. The monitor flickered and then a thin red line appeared just below the video editor. It jumped and then flatlined. Then it jumped again. And again and again, until it began to resemble a heartbeat.

"It's recording!" Bob yelled.

Nina looked up. The Frankenstein monster held his creator by his neck. Herr Frankenstein beat the monster about the face and head. Fritz swayed from his chain noose. They were all glowing in the white haze.

Herr Frankenstein's eyes rolled back into his head and his arms went limp by his side. The mon-ster continued to shake the dead body.

Then they all began to fade — Fritz, Herr Franken-stein, and the monster.

A nuclear explosion of lightning blinded Nina,

Joe, and Bob and they turned away from the searing light. When it had passed, they all turned to discover that the trio had disappeared. The chains and the platform swung in the cool breeze like chimes on a back porch.

Joe hit the EJECT button and the CD drawer slid out. He took the CD from its tray and held it in his hands.

"Time to put these three back where they belong," he said.

A groan filled the room.

Nina ran to Detective Turner, who was still sprawled where the monster had hit him. "Are you okay?"

Turner sat up slowly, wobbling. "Yeah. It's been a tough week."

"Hey, Trey," Bob said as he walked up to his lab partner, who was lying near a gurney. "How you feeling?"

Trey sat up and rubbed the side of his head.

"Man," Bob said, "you look like a bowling ball."

"You ought to see yourself, *mi amigo*," Trey said with a slight smile. "You look like a coconut."

"Well," Nina added with a devilish smile, "you got the *nut* part right."

Bob frowned while Joe stifled a laugh. "How you feeling?" Bob asked Trey again.

"I do not know, homey." Trey rubbed the side of his head again. "I have a very bad headache."

"Hey!" came a shout.

They all jumped. It was Oscar, struggling against the leather straps that held him down. "One of you underclassmen want to untie me from this table?"

Bob walked over to the helpless Oscar. He smiled.

"C'mon, cue ball," Oscar demanded. "Let me out of here."

Bob rubbed his newly shorn head. "Hey, Trey, you know what *noogies* are?"

Trey joined Bob at the table. "No, homey. What is a *noogie?*"

"Oh, brother," Nina moaned.

"Don't you dare," Oscar said through gritted teeth.

Bob held up his right hand and clenched his fist. Then he uncurled his first two fingers just enough that the joints stood out like crags.

"I'm warning you, *freshman!*" Oscar said, struggling against his bindings.

"Do this," Bob said, showing Trey his right hand.

Trey made the same fist as Bob.

"Noogies are an age-old tradition here in San Tomas. It's the way we welcome newcomers to our fair little village. It's sort of a way of saying, 'We're glad you're here.'" Bob looked down at Oscar. "We're glad you're here," he said, and began rubbing Oscar's head with his crooked fingers.

"Ow!" Oscar shouted. "That burns."

"Groovy," Trey said, his eyes dancing. He began rubbing Oscar's head, too.

"Owwwww!"

"Freshmen," Nina moaned.

CHAPTER TWENTY-FIVE

FRIDAY, 7 P.M.
DETECTIVE TURNER'S HOME

Trey gobbled the last of his chili dog and then burped. "Excuse me," he said, reddening. "Mexican food gives me gas."

"Pull my finger," Bob told Trey.

"Huh?" Trey said, perplexed.

Bob held out his finger.

"Don't do it, Trey," Nina pleaded.

Too late. Trey pulled Bob's finger and Bob belched loud and long. Bob frowned and then said, "Yeech. I don't remember eating that!"

"Oh, gross," Nina said, waving the air in front of her. "What have you eaten today?"

"Burritos for lunch and chili dogs for dinner," Bob said proudly. "A good ol'-fashioned American meal."

"Let me know when you're ready," Joe said. He was kneeling by Turner's entertainment center. He tapped the tray of the DVD player and it slowly slid inside.

"I can't stay too long," Nina said. "I've got to get up early tomorrow."

"On Saturday?" Bob said. "Isn't that against the Geneva Convention or something?"

"You're the only one at war with life, Captain Bob," Nina said with a smirk. "I've got to get down to the convention center and help set up the Egyptian exhibit."

"Ready when you are," Turner said from his lounge chair. He spoke with his mouth full of chili dog.

"Am I the only one in this room with manners?" Nina said, a disgusted look on her face.

Bob belched out a "yes" and then smiled.

"*Freshmen,*" Nina groaned. The she smiled. At least she would be able to tease Captain Bob about his bald head for a while. The light gleamed off the top of his smooth pate.

Turner grinned at Bob and Trey. "You guys better be careful at school. I understand Oscar's looking to add some knots to both of your heads."

"Everything is okay," Trey said. "Gloria told Oscar's grandmother about his bad manners and bad grades in school. So now he must apologize and work every day after school until his grades are better. Gloria is tutoring him."

"Hey, there they are," Joe said, pointing at the screen.

Herr Frankenstein and Fritz were digging in a graveyard, removing a coffin and then carting it off. They stopped at a gallows, cut down a recently hanged criminal, and added his body to their cart.

"I think I like the movie better than reality," Trey said. He rubbed the side of his head. "I do not like the idea of my brain being so exposed."

"That was quite a brainstorm Joe had," Bob said. "I didn't know what to do when the camera wouldn't work."

"Herr Frankenstein had adapted to modern technology," Joe said. "That was the only way to defeat him."

"What about the camera?" Nina said. "If it no longer works, how are we going to defeat the next monster?"

"Next monster?" Trey said, his eyes wide with fear. "There are more monsters to defeat?"

"Three more," Bob said.

"I think I will go back to Cuba," Trey said, a serious look on his face. "There are too many monsters in America, homey."

Bob snorted a laugh and Turner choked on his chili dog. Nina just rolled her eyes. But Joe didn't notice. He was too wrapped up in the sad tale of Herr Frankenstein and his Creature.

EPILOGUE
LATER THAT NIGHT

Joe sat at his computer, typing in his journal. He would finish up the details of the battle with Herr Frankenstein and his Creature and then check out his favorite web site. He wanted to read Captain Bob's version of their battle with the mad scientist. He liked reading Bob's stories. Bob was a good writer, so good that sometimes Joe liked the fictionalized accounts better than what had actually happened.

It didn't bother Joe that Bob's accounts of their battles with Count Dracula, the Wolf Man, and now Frankenstein were not entirely accurate. Joe understood his friend's desire for attention — good or bad. Joe was learning in his psychology class that some boys who grow up without a father often have vivid, creative imaginations; overexaggerate their own exploits; and even have short attention spans for tedious, everyday things.

Captain Bob was a textbook case.

Joe finished his journal, saved it, and decided to

just go to bed. He stretched, yawned, and rolled into bed.

Three down and three to go. Three more monsters. Which would be next? Which would be the next monster to rear its ugly head? And what would they do if the camera didn't work, just like Nina said?

Nina.

Joe sat up in bed.

Nina had to get up early to go help set up the Egyptian exhibit for the Western Civilization and Humanities Exhibition at the San Tomas Inlet Cultural Society.

An Egyptian exhibit complete with hieroglyphics, ancient papyrus scrolls, gold scarabs, pottery, and a sarcophagus.

A sarcophagus that contained a mummy.

Joe sat his alarm for seven A.M. He had just volunteered himself to help set up the exhibit with Nina. And while helping to set up the exhibit, he would investigate that sarcophagus just to make sure the mummy within was really dead.